The Vacuum Chamber

The Vacuum Chamber

Two Novellas

Ba'bila Mutia

Spears Books

Denver, Colorado

Spears Books
An Imprint of Spears Media Press LLC
7830 W. Alameda Ave, Suite 103-247
Denver, CO 80226
United States of America

First Published in the United States of America in 2021 by Spears Books
www.spearsmedia.com
info@spearsmedia.com
Information on this title: www.spearsmedia.com/the-vacuum-chamber
© 2021 Ba'bila Mutia
All rights reserved.

ISBN: 9781942876700 (Paperback)
ISBN: 9781942876724 (eBook)
Also available in Kindle format

Designed and typeset by Spears Media Press LLC
Cover designed by Doh Kambem
Cover Photo by Elti Meshau

Distributed globally by African Books Collective (ABC)
www.africanbookscollective.com

For Dayebga

Contents

The Vacuum Chamber

1

The Futuristic Institute of Science and Technology (FIST), as it came to be known, was rumoured to be hidden in the Mendankwe Mountains of the North-Western region of the country. In a country ridden with crime, endemic corruption, and election fraud, it was not surprising that Dr Tanda Matanda, the man claimed to be the Institute's director had become a mystery. The existence of the Institute itself, like the identity of Dr Matanda, was shrouded in rumour and obscurity.

The Institute would not have become renowned if the main opposition political party, the Front against Injustice of the State and Throat (FIST) did not have the same acronym as the Institute. FIST, the party, attained popularity partly by the immense appeal of its campaign slogan, 'Power to the People' and its famous clenched-fist salute which all its militants defiantly raised in the air during political rallies.

Before the early 90s, there was only one party in the country—the Collective National Union (CNU). The first head-of-state after independence, Papa Batoura, as the nation fondly came to call him, was the founder of the CNU. "Without one party, one people, one way of thinking, directed towards national unity in a country with more than three hundred ethnic groups, we cannot achieve peace, economic development and social harmony," he used to tell the nation over the state-owned national radio station. That's how the UPC, UC, KNDP, CPNC, KPP, and the rest of the political parties were suppressed to create the CNU with its motto "One People, One Party, One Nation."

Batoura's dictatorship became vicious and absolute. Anyone who spoke against the regime or who was suspected of having another way of thinking was immediately arrested and sent for interrogation and liquidation in one of the several underground prisons dotted all over the country. Under interrogation, 'traitors of the party' as the state-owned *Daily National Tribune* came to label them, provided names of their family members who thought like them. That's how it came to pass that friends and family members of 'traitors' were arrested and made to disappear.

Just before Batoura died of throat cancer, he handpicked Laupo Ayiba, his trusted Prime Minister, to replace him. To distance himself from Batoura's reign of terror, Ayiba quickly transformed the party into a people's movement—the People's Democratic Movement. "This is no longer a dictatorship," Ayiba used to proclaim in his raucous voice. "The PDM is a popular democratic movement. Anyone can stand for elections, even to be head-of-state." Everyone knew that these were mere words. The offices of the much-dreaded SEDOC, the secret police that Batoura had put into place, were still active, collecting and filing documentation on radical university lecturers, newspaper editors, deviant intellectuals, trade unionists, and political activists who were opposed to the new regime. The country had changed hands from Batoura to Ayiba, but the fear to have a different voice or state contrary opinions still haunted the nation.

It was against this backdrop that it was rumoured a new political party would be launched. Civil servants, students, lawyers, government ministers, trade unions, and magistrates staged protest marches against any opposition to PDM. Despite the threats of a bloody confrontation and a government crackdown, FIST was launched. Almost immediately, the regime registered five hundred political parties. Despite the 'advanced multi-party democracy', nothing really changed. The PDM government tolerated no opposing political ideology and no questions concerning oil revenues. Public or parliamentary inquiries on the military budget or salaries of members of the presidential guard were prohibited.

I dropped out from the state-owned school of journalism two years after FIST was launched. On three occasions, the government-appointed director of the school summoned me to his office and cautioned me about asking the kind of questions I asked in my classes. The first occasion was a mild rebuke about my challenging Dr Abega on "notions of independent reporting and investigative journalism." The director raised his right hand when I tried to justify my views. "You have still been a student, still wanting to learn," he said in appalling English. "You be English-speaking," he continued. "Do French-speaking students ask questions like di kind you de askam for class?"

"No, *Monsieur Le Directeur*," I said.

"*Voila*," he retorted. "I know you de comot for Bamenda. But please, be good Anglophone. No make much trouble."

I can't remember what provoked the second summons; but it was the third summons that indicated I had run into serious trouble with the school administration. The director was furious as soon as I walked into his office. He didn't even allow me to sit down. His usually mild face was contorted into a furious mask of rage.

"*Monsieur* Fondo," he exploded as soon as I stepped into his plush, carpeted office. "You must be a fool," he carried on in French. He was so mad that the remnant of broken English in his mind had virtually evaporated. I tried to say something, but he banged his right fist on the table. "Shut up!" he yelled. "I've worked for close to fifteen years to be where I'm today. I will not tolerate an idiot to ruin my hard-earned position in this system. You understand?"

"*Oui, Monsieur.* But what's wrong, *Monsieur*?" I was taken aback by his fury.

"You know what's wrong!" he shouted. "This institution is not a training ground for revolutionaries."

"*Mais, Monsieur Le Directeur —*"

"Shut up and listen to me! I have received reports from every lecturer in your department concerning your attitude in class. Do you know that there are government-paid informants who report what goes on here to the presidency? How dare you raise the kind of issues you provoked in *Monsieur* Oyono's class?"

"It wasn't a provocation, *Monsieur Le Directeur*. I simply wanted clarification on the abuse of state power and the citizen's right to know the truth."

"What truth?" he shouted back. "The presidency is the embodiment of truth in this country. There's no other truth. You didn't just end at that. You raised questions on journalists' access to information concerning oil revenues and the salary of the head-of-state. How dare you!"

"It's the right of reporters to ask questions like these to inform the public, *Monsieur*. That's what I tried to explain to Professor Oyono—"

"You're an idiot! The curriculum of this institution is meant to train journalists for the state-owned media. You constitute a danger to state opinion."

"Public opinion, *Monsieur Le Directeur*," I said.

He took out a handkerchief from his pocket and wiped the mixture of spittle and froth that had oozed from around the corners of his mouth and stained his goatee. He put back the handkerchief in his pocket. In what seemed to be a change of tactics, he peeled off the jacket of his charcoal grey suit and sat down. He struggled to contain his rage as his round puffy face lost some of its anger.

"Sit down," he continued in French, this time in a quieter voice.

I sat down.

"How old are you?"

"Twenty-three, *Monsieur* Le Directeur."

"What do your parents do for a living?"

"My father died when I was an infant, *Monsieur*. My mother is in the village. She's a subsistence farmer."

"I see." He stood up and went into the self-contained bathroom in his office. A moment later he emerged with a long rectangular mirror. He came over to where I sat, holding the mirror. "I want you to look at yourself in this mirror." He noticed the puzzled expression on my face as he sat down. "Go on, look at the mirror," he said.

"I don't understand, *Monsieur*—"

"Just do it!"

I took the mirror and stood up. I stole a glance at the figure that scowled back at me. I turned my face away and looked at the director.

"Well," he said, "what have you seen?"

"I have seen myself, *Monsieur*."

"Look more closely at your face, the clothes you're wearing. Take a hard honest appraisal of yourself and tell me exactly what you see."

I turned back to the mirror. The face I saw was haggard. I couldn't afford the money for a regular visit to the barbers. My hair was unkempt. What was supposed to be a youthful face had become furrowed with lines of worry and weariness. My *okrika*[1] shirt was without two buttons. It was rough and un-ironed. The jeans trousers I wore hung loosely on my waist, without a belt. The trousers were old and faded. The soles of my black second-hand shoes were worn thin. The shoes themselves were cracked. I didn't wear socks.

"Yes?" the director said, tapping an impatient tattoo with the fingers of his left hand on his office table, "I'm listening."

"Not a very good picture of myself," I said.

"Okay." He stood up and said, "Let me have the mirror." He took the mirror to the bathroom, came back, and sat down behind his table.

"I admire your honesty, *Monsieur* Fondo. Not many people can confront themselves the way you've done and say exactly what they've seen in the mirror. What you've seen in the mirror is actually the nation as it is today. You're the nation. The nation is you. You're what the mirror reflects back, and you deserve what you see. Do you understand?"

"No, *Monsieur*. If I understand you well—"

"If my memory serves me right, I remember you came first in the competitive entrance exam in your batch. Am I

[1] Used, secondhand

6

right?"

"You're right, *Monsieur*."

"You're a very smart young man who could have served this government with dedication. You're the kind of young men we need to build this nation. But you've forced us to think otherwise. You have a very long way to go, Monsieur Fondo, a very long way."

"And what do you think about what I said in Dr Oyono's class, *Monsieur Le Directeur*?"

"You can go now. I'm finished with you."

I tried to say something, but he didn't look up again. He just went on as if there wasn't anyone in his office. I stood up, went out of the office and closed the door behind me.

Two months later, when the results of the second semester exams were put up on the departmental notice board, I was shocked to discover I had failed six out of seven courses. I was convinced there was some kind of mistake. I had always topped my class right from the first year. I tried to see my lecturers, but no one would receive me. I went back to the director's office several times to book an appointment to see him, but his secretary always said he was in one meeting or another. It took about a month for me to figure out what had happened. My initial aspiration to work with the state-owned media was now a dead dream. At the end of the year, I withdrew from the school.

2

That is how I picked up a job with *The Daily Mirror*, a private-owned paper. The salary was comfortable. I could now afford good clothes and regular meals. I looked and felt good. It took me only a year to establish a reputation as the best investigative journalist in the country. From the several letters the paper received each week from our readers, my weekly column, *The Face behind the Iron Mask*, was the most widely read column in any newspaper in the country.

One of my initial desires was to find out whether Dr Matanda and the Futuristic Institute really existed. I was also carrying out a parallel investigation on any direct or remote links between FIST (the Institute) and FIST (the party). It was quite obvious that Dr Matanda had gripped the popular imagination of the nation. It was my responsibility to provide evidence that he actually existed and was not just a myth, a creation of the people's collective imagination. All leads to Dr Matanda or the Institute led to dead ends. A couple of leads turned out to be hoaxes. But why was there a lot of information on the grapevine about the Institute? Did it actually exist? What kind of research was the purported Dr Matanda carrying on?

I began my investigation by consulting the Internet. I was surprised to find more than forty-five entries with the name

Matanda. Matanda was not exclusively an African name. People in unrelated places as far away as Thailand, China, Brazil, Puerto Rico, and Argentina were named Matanda. Quite by chance I came across one T. Matanda who had been at M.I.T. in the eighties. The only available information on the website was that T. Matanda was a graduate student who had conducted advanced research on particle physics. No additional information was provided. There was no clear link between T. Matanda and Dr Tanda Matanda. After a few more searches I gave up.

As time went by, my initial enthusiasm of unveiling the mystery surrounding Dr Matanda and his alleged Institute gradually fizzled out. Common sense told me Dr Matanda did not exist. He had been fabricated by the imagination of a people yearning for political change. But my investigative instinct, something deep inside me, kept on nudging me that the numerous stories about Dr Tanda Matanda were based on some kind of reality, albeit ambiguous and vague.

That's how I began covering FIST rallies in my attempt to clutch at any straw that would lead me to Dr Tanda Matanda. I needed a story. And I was becoming desperate to get one, no matter the cost. My initial assessment was that FIST (the party) wanted people to think differently and not, for example, be forced to watch the State-owned TV or listen to the one o'clock state-owned radio news in which appointments in government were made. I recall one rally, in which the party's charismatic leader, Jani Frandi, whipped up the emotion of the crowd with his acerbic, sometimes unsympathetic rhetoric.

"Do you consider this system a democracy in which university rectors, cabinet ministers, even prime ministers are appointed and dismissed over the radio?"

"Noooooo!" the crowd roared.

"Do you call this a democracy in which we all have to look at the world through the same coloured eyeglasses?"

"Noooooo!" the crowd yelled again.

"Is there justice in a system in which the citizens have no idea about how much their head-of- state earns, how much revenue our oil fetches, how much soldiers of the presidential guard earn?"

"Noooooo!"

Jani Frandi was slowly but gradually driving the crowd to frenzy. A short smile hovered momentarily around the corners of his tight-lipped, contemptuous mouth.

"Who are we?" his voice bellowed over the huge loudspeakers.

"The people!" the crowd roared back.

"Who are the people?"

"We are the people."

"What do we want?" Jani Frandi bellowed at the crowd.

Ten thousand people punched their clenched fists in the air and screamed in a thunderous, electrifying frenzy, "Power!"

"What power?"

Again the thousands of people in the crowd raised their fists in the air and shouted back, "People power! Power to the people!"

"Hey krujay!"

"Heeeeeey!" the crowd roared back.

"Krujay!"

"Heeeeeey!"

"One time—"

"Hmmmmm!"

As time passed and FIST was voted into parliament, the party began to lose steam. The first thing FIST MPs did as soon as they got into parliament was to use the micro project funds that were meant to develop their constituencies to buy flamboyant four-wheel drive vehicles. They became drunk with money and power they had only imagined in their wildest dreams. When parliament was not in session and they returned to their constituencies, they became conceited and kept themselves aloof from the people that had voted them into parliament. The party's once mesmerizing slogan 'power to the people' was reduced to a mere catchphrase that had lost its original appeal.

It is these thoughts that ran through my mind as I made my way to the bank to pick up my September salary. The taxi I was in crept slowly past *Marché Central*. During pay days like this, the downtown area was crammed with endless lines of cars, mostly yellow taxicabs. I glanced at my watch and realized I had only fifteen more minutes before the bank closed.

"Listen," I said in French to the taxi man, "I barely have fifteen more minutes before my bank closes. With these long traffic jams, I don't think I'll make it to the bank. And today is Friday."

"You better get down then," he said as he swung the car to the right and stopped near the pavement. "But you still have to pay the full fare."

"No problem," I said. I brought out two hundred francs from my pocket and paid the full fare. Then I began running down the street, weaving in and out of the traffic like a mad man. I was gasping for air when I got to the bank.

11

There were just five minutes left before the doors would be closed. As usual, there was an assortment of vendors selling made-in-china radios, calculators, and toothbrushes. Others sold mobile phone cards, pirated compact discs, used shoes, groundnuts, school bags, and bananas. The vendors and their wares were endless, unlimited. Long queues of people, mostly civil servants, lined up patiently inside the bank to collect their meagre salaries or apply for overdrafts. The air in the bank was stuffy with cheap perfumes and the armpit sweat of desperate but enduring people. It took me close to two hours before I picked up my salary. Like the rest of the population, I could not afford savings. I cleaned out my account as soon as my monthly salary reached the bank.

I was exhausted, hungry, and thirsty as I left the bank through the back entrance. I crossed the road, descended a flight of stairs, and made my way down to one of the generic roadside restaurants that specialize in roast fish, chicken, and fried ripe plantains. I ordered a plate of roast chicken drumsticks, fried ripe plantains, and a beer. It did not take long for my order to come. As I ate, I looked at the faces around me. They were characterized by unarticulated despair and enduring desolation born out of boredom and the aimless existence of individuals resigned to their fate. I brought out my notebook and, in between mouthfuls, began jotting down my observations. I listened to a small group of four men and one woman around a table next to mine. They did not appear to know each other. They spoke and ate without thinking, moving from one subject of conversation to the next—the most recent cabinet reshuffle; a woman in Douala who had transformed into a snake after making love to a man; a driver in the presidential guard who was rumoured to have eloped with a minister's wife; the latest statistics on AIDS in the country; the upcoming parliamentary elections; eight members of the country's Olympic team who had disappeared in Dubai; an accident on the Yaoundé-Douala highway involving a Chinese-made motorbike and a drunken army colonel whose trunk was loaded with one hundred million francs of counterfeit currency; a train derailment in Eseka that had killed more than one hundred people. When I finished eating I paid my bill, stood up, and climbed the steps back to the street.

It was there that I saw a large crowd of mostly men surround an itinerant herbalist who had set camp on the sidewalk across the street. I crossed the street, stood at the edge of the crowd, and joined the curious onlookers. The herbalist was a diminutive, middle-aged man dressed in an old loincloth and a faded multi-coloured jumper. He sat on a carved stool with the impassive features of his ancient face staring nonchalantly at the crowd. He smoked a pipe whose smoke rose lazily into the humid afternoon air. It was his apprentice who held the crowd spellbound. He was a much younger man in his twenties who had a python slithering lazily round his neck. The pavement in front of the duo was littered with several bottles of herbal concoctions—snake oils, carved human statutes, a black clay pot, and barks of trees. A signboard by the roadside indicated the concoctions cured syphilis, erectile dysfunction, AIDS, stomach problems, hepatitis, liver and kidney difficulties, and countless other disorders. The apprentice rang a bell and uttered some arcane incantations each time he moved and bowed his head in front of a carved statue. The crowd waited impatiently for the ritual to end before the sale of the herbal concoctions would begin.

I wanted to ask a few questions on their claim to cure AIDS so I too waited for the sale of their herbal portions to start. I barely noticed two men approach the crowd. I felt uncomfortable when they edged nearer and sandwiched me. As I tried to move aside, they gripped me on both hands.

"Don't shout or attract any attention to yourself." It was a command. I felt the warm breath of the man in my ear. "We don't wish to harm you. Please just do as we say."

My first instinct was that they were pickpockets who had tailed me all the way from the bank and now wanted to take away my entire month's salary.

"Who are you? What do you want?" I barely caught a glance of their beefy muscular torsos and bulging biceps. I tried to shake them off.

"Don't make this difficult for us—" the second man started to say.

I had to get out of their grip. If everything else failed, I heard myself thinking, I would shout for help. I raised my right foot and brought it down with all force on the black shoe of the man on my right. I heard him grunt as his grip on my right hand slackened momentarily. I made an attempt to wrench myself free from the second man. No one in the crowd seemed to notice what was going on. Out of the corner of my eye, I saw the first man bring out a handkerchief from his pocket. Everything happened so quickly after that. He stuffed my nose and mouth with the handkerchief. I smelled an unusual, upsetting odour as I felt myself lifted effortlessly from the pavement and carried away. The last two thoughts I had before I lost consciousness were: *they must be very powerful men to lift me up in the air like that* and *how will I live without my salary for this month?*

3

I was at the bottom of a lake or an ocean, trying to float to the surface without success. I tried several times. After a while I felt myself rise slowly but surely to the surface as my breathing got easier. The first thing I heard before I opened my eyes was the monotonous drone of a powerful car engine. When I opened my eyes, I realized it was night and I was in a moving car. The powerful headlights of the car illuminated the rapidly receding highway as the car sped along the dark tarmac. I felt slightly dizzy. My attention came back to the car. The dark silhouettes of a driver and another man were in front of the car. I was seated behind the driver and restrained by a seatbelt. I looked to my right and saw another shape, this time of a short thickset man with glasses and a suit. I could not see his face properly. His head rested on the back seat of the car's leather upholstery. It was hard to tell whether he was awake or asleep. My first thought was that state security agents had kidnapped me. I thought about all the articles that had appeared in my weekly column. There was nothing I had written for a long time that was seditious to have upset the regime.

"Why have I been kidnapped?" I heard myself ask. "Where are you taking me to?"

The short stocky man in the suit beside me lifted his head

and turned in my direction. "Mr Fondo," he said, "let me apologise. We don't mean you any harm. By the way, good morning." He stretched his hand in my direction.

"I refuse to shake hands with people I don't know."

"I understand," he said in a composed, apologetic voice. "I don't blame you. I would react the same way under these unusual circumstances. Please don't take offence. I had no other choice."

"I demand some explanation of what's going on. I need to know where I am."

"In my car, of course," the man responded rather humorously.

"I know I'm in a car." My voice was harsh and sarcastic. "And who the hell are you?"

"Matanda," he said. "Dr Tanda Matanda."

"Is this some kind of joke?"

"Not at all, Mr Fondo. I'm Tanda Matanda. You're the famous reporter of *The Daily Mirror*, I presume. I'm an ardent reader of your column, *The Face behind the Iron* Mask. You've been trying to provide evidence about my existence for more than a year now, if I'm not mistaken."

"You can't be Dr Tanda Matanda!"

A smile lingered on the shadowy features of his face. "Well, you'll soon find out for yourself. I don't need to authenticate my own existence. Let me take this chance to introduce Jean-Bosco my driver and Lipenja who happens to be my bodyguard."

I glanced at my watch. "It can't be four thirty! How long have I been unconscious?"

"The time is correct. We left Yaoundé at ten in the night. My men had no choice than to use the mild anaesthesia on the handkerchief. The dose wasn't enough. We had to inject you with another long-lasting dose. I can't afford to take risks, particularly when I leave the Institute and come out in person to the open."

"The Institute of Futuristic Inquiry into Science and Technology?"

"That's correct." Another brief smile hovered momentarily on his face. "We shall get to the Institute at dawn."

I was now wide awake. I touched my jacket and felt the money I had collected from the bank.

"Your money is intact, Mr Fondo. We're not pickpockets."

"You must have looked at my ID," I went on. "That's how you know my name."

"Negative," he said. "You've been observed for more than a year. You dropped out from the National School of Journalism before you became a journalist with the private press. You fell afoul of the state-run administration because of your personal views in the school, right?"

"Right," I said.

He smiled again. "I have more surprises for you, Mr Fondo."

"What does the Institute look like, Dr Matanda?"

"Ah, I see you've overcome your initial scepticism about who I am."

"I'm a professional journalist, Dr Matanda. I trust my instincts."

"I would think so. And your imagination too, I presume. The human imagination is the mind's eye. Instinct cannot exist without imagination, Mr Fondo."

"I'd like to deduce that T. Matanda who was a graduate student at M.I.T. in the early 80s and Dr Tanda Matanda are

17

one and the same person."

"Indeed, they are. I'm quite aware that you've been searching for me."

"I gather your area of graduate research was in particle physics, actually in particle acceleration and force field
generation."

"Well?" he hesitated. "There's more to it than what my
academic records at M.I.T. indicate. It's a little bit compli-
cated. We'll talk about it when we get to the Institute."

At about four thirty, the car slowed down as it came
to a junction somewhere after Mendankwe. The driver left
the main highway and turned on a narrow dirt road to the
right. The bumpy and potholed nature of the road reduced
the speed of the car considerably. The landscape had become
hillier. The driver changed to second gear as the car ascended
the steep hills. We kept on driving for another twenty-five
minutes as the first light of dawn began creeping over the
horizon. It was then I noticed that we were driving through a
small village. The sparse habitation among the hills indicated
a population of about a hundred inhabitants. Dr Matanda
said the village was called Mbekakum and was the last habitation before we reached the mountains. The Institute was
another forty-five minutes' drive up the precarious terrain.
The climb became steeper as the car made its way along the
narrow ledge of a road. I looked at my watch. It was getting
to five in the morning. There were steep ravines and cliffs of
about two kilometres deep on both sides of the winding road.
A stranger could not drive up here. The car made a left turn
and slowed down to a stop. The car's headlights illuminated
two huge boulders of about twenty-five metres in diameter
in front of us. The road had suddenly come to an abrupt end.

I turned and looked at Dr Matanda.

"The road has come to an end," I said in a shaky voice, thinking the driver had made a mistake and come up the wrong mountain road. "And there's no way to turn back. What are we going to do?"

"Nothing," Dr Matanda said. "The road continues."

I failed to understand what he meant for I could see no road. I found myself at the edge of the car seat anxiously watching the driver. The driver pushed a combination of black and red knobs and entered a code on a numbered keyboard on an electronic gadget much like the size of a large calculator attached on the dashboard of the car. I had not noticed the gadget on the dashboard. That was when I became aware that the car was a Mercedes, a black Mercedes. I looked again at Dr Matanda. He was calm and unperturbed. A few minutes later I felt the car vibrate as it was shaken by an uninterrupted tremor from inside the mountains. The tremor continued. It was accompanied by an unrelenting hum. Right in front of my eyes, I saw the two boulders part. They moved apart slowly to reveal a road that continued into the mountains. I looked at Dr Matanda. I was too dumbfounded to say anything.

The same vague smile hung on his face. "I told you the road continues."

We drove for another ten minutes and the driver brought the car to a halt. He came out of the car. Dr Matanda too came out. The other man stayed in the car. Out of curiosity, I too came out.

"It's here that the road actually comes to an end," Dr Matanda said rather unceremoniously.

"I don't understand," I said. "I can see the road in front

of me."

"In a sense you're right. There seems to be a road, but in reality there's no road because we can't drive through what appears to be the road."

I felt more confused than ever. The driver went to the trunk of the car as we spoke, opened it, and came back with a black metallic briefcase. He handed it to Dr Matanda. Matanda opened the briefcase and placed it on top of the car's trunk. I came closer and looked inside the briefcase. From the outside it seemed to be an ordinary briefcase. But when I looked inside I realized it was a complex electronic box with buttons, dials, switches, and an array of electronic components I had never seen before. Matanda operated on the electronic box for about two minutes. All of a sudden, I perceived a strange pulsating sound. It was hardly perceptible. It went on for about five minutes, and then a kind of brilliant burst of white light appeared in the emerging dawn of the sky above us. The pulsating vibrations died down steadily. Matanda pushed a series of buttons on the electronic briefcase and then closed it gently. He gave it to the driver to put it back into the trunk.

"We can continue the drive now," Dr Matanda said. We entered the car. The driver came back to his seat, started the engine and continued driving. I did not notice anything unusual.

"What was that all about?" I inquired.

"It's hard to give an explanation right away. I'll explain things later on in the day or tomorrow when the chance presents itself." There was a trace of weariness in his voice. It had been a long night and I felt he didn't want to answer further questions.

We began the slow descent to the Institute at six fifteen. I had a chance now to look at Dr Matanda more closely. He was a short thickset man with a jovial rotund face. He was clean shaven, and the hair on top of his head was already receding into baldness. Little tuffs of hair could be seen protruding out of his ears and nostrils. His puffy cheeks vibrated as he spoke. His glasses, which were much thicker than my initial assessment, put him across as a methodical and organized man dedicated to scientific inquiry. As the car continued its descent, the narrow mountain road merged into a broad cobblestone street with culverts on both sides. Down below a valley I saw buildings of assorted shapes—several bungalows, L-shaped structures, and a dome shaped building. I also saw gardens, hedges, and trees. From the distance the buildings looked methodical, interspersed with concrete paths and green lawns.

"The Institute looks quite impressive from up here," I remarked, turning my attention to Dr Matanda.

"You think so? I've done everything to make the place feel like home. Actually, the Institute is spread out across a number of valleys separated by small hills within a much larger basin. You can't see everything from here. The entire basin covers about five by ten kilometres. The remarkable geographical wonder is that the basin is completely surrounded by the mountains, making it an inaccessible fortress."

"How did you discover this place?"

"Quite by chance," Dr Matanda said. "When I was in the Ministry, I was in the habit of roaming the countryside, searching for crystals and stones with a particular structure I knew existed in this country. I was quite certain that such a find would be useful for particle acceleration. I was told of a strange rock in the mountainous region of Mendankwe, somewhere in a remote village. Then one weekend I met a trader in the Pinyin market who had samples of this strange rock. He had only a few broken fragments. I bought them from him and returned to Yaoundé. An analysis of the rocks in the lab revealed the unique crystal structure was the one I had been searching for all these years.

"I went back to the Pinyin market where I had met the trader. He had not been seen for three market weeks. No one seemed to know his name or what compound he came from. Month after month, for up to six months, I kept on going back to Pinyin to no avail. The man had simply disappeared. It was getting close to Christmas, and I was going to my village. It was on a Saturday, around the *Mitajem* toll gate, that I heard it was the Pinyin market day. I don't know what made me make the detour to Pinyin. There he was, when I got to the market! Tears ran down my eyes when I saw him. His first thought was that I had lost someone in my family.

"No, no," I lied. "I think I have a terrible headache."

"The stone will cure the headache," he said. "Just press it to the front and back of your head twice a day. You'll be okay on the third day."

"Do you have additional pieces of the rock?" I asked him, as I wiped the two streams of tears on my cheeks with the back of my left hand.

"Yes," he said. "I have many of them. They were washed down by the rain." He emptied a small wicker basket on the ground in front of him. There were several large pieces that appeared to have been part of a much larger rock.

"I came to gather that he was actually a smuggler who did brisk business selling gunpowder and shotgun cartridges from Nigeria. Unlike most smugglers who moved in large groups at night through the forest, he was a lone ranger who preferred the mountain passes in the daytime to evade surprise custom raids. He told me he had picked up the strange stone as he trekked across a valley in the mountains. He had discovered a narrow pass through the mountains on a footpath that wound up the slopes of a village called Mbekakum. It was the unusual azure colour of the crystals that made him pick them up and sell them in the market. The village, as I later came to find out, was an isolated settlement that did not even exist on the map.

"Seven months later, after several failed rendezvous with the trader, both of us finally met and journeyed to Mbekakum. We went up the mountain pass he mentioned and came to this marvellous place you see spread out in front of us. *Calactamalamite*, that's the name of the crystal, abounded in huge quantities in the rock formation of the mountains. Six months later I resigned from the Ministry and disappeared from the national scene. With the help of some trusted Mbekakum locals, I came up here and began mining crystals from the rock. Within two years I constructed a makeshift lab to process the crystals into components I would use to build the particle accelerator."

"And what about the trader?"

"You'll meet him later on in the day at the Institute."

The driver brought the car to a halt in the garage of Dr Matanda's main residence. I came out of the garage and stood outside. The front entrance to the house had a beautiful green lawn surrounded by rectangular formations of bachelor buttons, marigolds, roses, and a variety of lovely flowers whose delicate scent assailed my nostrils.

Dr Matanda said, "Jean-Bosco, my driver, will take you to the guest quarters. Please make yourself comfortable. You'll find everything you may need in the apartment—toothpaste and brushes, deodorants, towels, pyjamas, underwear, shirts, trousers, slippers, jogging shoes and sandals of various sizes and colours that will fit. We'll have a late brunch at about eleven. There is an alarm clock by your bedside, if you need to rest. I suggest you set it at ten. Good morning and see you later."

Jean-Bosco escorted me to the guest quarters, showed me into my room, and left. The bed in the room was made up with clean multi-coloured sheets, a thick cosy blanket, and two pillows. I removed my shoes and socks and took off my tie and jacket. I set the alarm clock at ten and fell down with exhaustion on the bed.

4

The alarm clock woke me up at ten. I got up, went to the bathroom, brushed my teeth and had a refreshing shower. I came back to the room and began searching the wardrobe for something to wear. The clothes were arranged in neat piles. I located a blue jogging suit with white stripes and tried it on. It was rather loose but felt fine. I tried about three pairs of tennis shoes before the third pair, brown in colour, fitted my feet. I went to the second window of the room through which sunlight was struggling to come in and pulled the curtains open. Sunlight flooded the whole room. I glanced at my watch as I strapped it to my wrist. It was getting close to ten forty-five. I opened the door and came out of the room. Jean-Bosco was there waiting for me.

"Morning, sir."

"Good morning, Jean-Bosco."

"This way, sir. Please, come with me. The doctor is waiting."

I looked around as I followed Jean-Bosco. The guest quarters were linked to Dr Matanda's main house by a long corridor adorned on both sides with a beautiful hedge. I turned around briefly to look at the guest quarters. The guest rooms were actually one rectangular building that contained the individual rooms and apartments. We went down a flight of stairs and turned left. Jean-Bosco opened a door, held it open and asked me to go in.

Dr Matanda stood up as I entered the room. "I hope the short sleep was refreshing, Mr Fondo."

"Oh, it was. And I actually enjoyed my shower too. I didn't realize how exhausted I was." The room was small with a rectangular dining table and six chairs. There was a small glass cupboard to the left that contained teacups, saucers, plates, and glasses. I noticed a black file on one side of the dining table. The room had only one window.

Dr Matanda glanced at the jogging suit I wore. "Looks funny," he said, "but the sneakers look great. Do they fit?"

"They fit perfectly. The jogging suit is a little loose, but it feels wonderful."

"Perhaps you'll like to go jogging after breakfast. We don't serve heavy breakfasts here. A little exercise will do you no harm."

"No, thanks. I'm not much of a jogger. I prefer tennis."

"Unfortunately, I don't have a tennis court in the Institute. I've never been a tennis fan. Over here," he said, waving me to a seat. "Breakfast will be ready in a moment." As he spoke, a lean old man came into the dining room from an adjoining door I guessed led into a kitchen. His shoulders stooped slightly. He had a dark, weather-beaten face with two furrowed lines proportionally etched on both sides of his small mouth. He wore a white apron and a chef's cap on his grey head. Dr Matanda helped him with the tray in which he carried glasses, plates, knives, forks, and cloth napkins.

As the man put the breakfast material on the table Dr Matanda said, "Let me introduce Mr Kuma Tah. He's both cook and gardener in the premises."

The old man acknowledged the introduction with a slight nod. "Good morning, Mr Fondo," he said in a deep resonant voice. "Welcome to the Institute."

As the old man took the tray and left the room, Matanda added: "He's the gunpowder smuggler I met in the Pinyin market. It's thanks to him that I found this place."

"How long has Kuma Tah been here with you?"

"Oh, about twenty-five years, if my memory serves me right."

"He must have been in his forties when he came here."

"He was forty-three to be more precise."

Kuma Tah returned with a tray of avocado, beetroot, lettuce, tomato, and grated carrot salad. He shuffled to the kitchen and came back with fresh strawberries, pumpkin muffins, whole wheat banana bread, and freshly squeezed pineapple and carrot juices.

"Please," Dr Matanda said, "*bon appétit.*"

I began with the salad and muffins. As we began eating, Matanda stretched his hand and pulled a black file toward him. He opened the file and looked at me. "With your permission, Mr Fondo, can I verify some details about you?"

"From that file?"

"Yes."

"Well, go ahead. But you know I also have questions to ask about your background, why you left the Ministry, the nature of the experiments you're conducting here in the mountains, and why you brought me here."

"I'll answer all your questions. I have nothing to hide." He turned his attention to the file and said, "Your full names are Gideon Nuvala Fondo, is that right?"

"That's correct."

"I'm interested in tracing the development of your imagination. I gather your father died when you were still an infant."

"Yes, that's correct."

"Your mother is still alive. She's a local farmer, isn't she?"

"Yes, she is."

"A Mill Hill missionary priest, Rev. Father Eckhart Breitinger, took you in his care and paid your fees in St. Francis boarding school. Is that right?"

"Yes."

"I understand Father Breitinger played both a violin and a harpsichord. Did you learn to play these musical instruments?"

"I did. Father Breitinger taught me how to play both of them. He used to say that music was essential in the development of the mind and the imagination." A sparkle of excitement appeared momentarily on Matanda's face when I mentioned the word 'imagination.' I saw him make a brief note in the file with his pen. "Apart from being an excellent player of local drums, I had never played these musical instruments before."

"But you mastered them, nonetheless. How long did it take you to learn them?"

"Under three months."

"Incredible! That's an amazing feat!"

"I remember Father Breitinger telling the other white missionaries that this was a rare achievement for an African boy of my age."

"Father Breitinger wanted you to become a priest?"

"I declined going to the seminary. I had always wanted to be a journalist. After my Advanced Levels, I wrote and passed the competitive entrance exam to the National School of Journalism."

"You came first on the entrance list, I gather."

"I did, yes. Well, you know the rest of the story."

"One more detail, Mr Fondo. Your file indicates a drop in grades in the first semester of your third year in secondary school. You were an A student throughout. But your grades dropped to B and C. What happened?"

I stopped speaking for a minute or two. Matanda was just raising a glass of carrot juice to his lips. He had not anticipated my silence. The glass was suspended briefly in mid-air before he placed it back on the table. He wanted to say something but thought it wise to hold his tongue.

"I've never spoken to anyone about the experiences that brought about the drop in my grades."

"Experiences?"

"You'll not believe what I'm about to tell you, Dr Matanda. I used to have strange nightly visitations with my late father. I don't know whether to call them dreams or visions. Hardly had I closed my eyes when I went to sleep than he appeared. I'm sure it was in full consciousness that I journeyed with him to cities I had never seen in my life. I spent most of my time in the day attempting to capture the memories of these amazing celestial cities in a notebook. I could no longer focus on my studies. And this lasted the entire semester."

"Amazing! Quite amazing!"

"My father's nightly visits stopped at the end of the semester, one week before we went on holidays. They ceased as suddenly as they had begun. His departure left me with a hollow feeling that I feel till this day. I later on used the material in the notebook to write supernatural short stories that were published as a collection by Simon & Schuster."

Matanda seemed to be taken by surprise. "You mean to say you're a published writer? I don't have this detail in your file! I haven't seen or heard about your collection of short stories. The Ministry of Secondary Education should have put the collection on the school reading list."

"It's used in teaching creative writing courses in the UK, Ireland, and the U.S.," I said. "And while we're talking about education, I'd like to know about your research at M.I.T, why you left the Ministry, and what exactly you do here."

"M.I.T. is a long time ago, but it all seems like yesterday. I'll try and be brief. After acquiring an MSc in Physics from the University of Ibadan, I obtained a PhD admission into M.I.T. in 1980 on a full scholarship to read Physics. My high school teacher and mentor in those days was the legendary and eccentric Dr Bokossa, whom everyone thought was slightly crazy.

"When I got to M.I.T. I decided to specialise in particle physics after my comprehensive exams. My supervisor was Professor Stanislaw McCloud, one of the finest brains at M.I.T. He was then chair of the Physics department and head of the M.I.T. scientific research team. He was the one who urged me to focus my research on 'Particle Acceleration.' Because of the cold war, the United States military was putting a lot of pressure on universities and private industries to research on non-conventional defence systems. Professor McCloud's theory was that energy generated from the collision of photons could be harnessed to create a force field which could not be penetrated by bombs or ballistic missiles. His peers scoffed at his wild fantasies and he soon became a pariah in university research establishments. Realizing my unusual ability in particle physics and the ease with which I solved equations, Professor McCloud urged me to narrow my theoretical investigations on 'Particle Acceleration and Force Field Generation' in the likelihood that the breakthrough that had eluded him all these years would come from an African brain. I used to work on the terminal of a mainframe located in a storage room which the Physics department had converted into an office for me.

"After five years of working day and night, I finally made the breakthrough. I had solved the equations that revealed that energy released from colliding photons could be harnessed to produce a force field. I didn't tell my supervisor about the breakthrough. I wanted the year to come to an end before I announced my discovery and apply to defend my PhD thesis. I think Professor McCloud must have seen the excitement and unusual change on my face. He knew something had happened, but he never asked me anything.

"One Friday evening, I came to my office and discovered that my lock had been picked and someone had broken into my computer room. Apparently, nothing had been stolen from the office. I switched on my terminal and interrogated the computer to bring up my files. Only a blank screen stared at me. The computer kept on saying the files did not exist. Experts from the computer science department did everything to search for the files to no avail. All the equations I had been working on for five years had simply vanished.

"Six months later, I came across a research paper on particle acceleration and force field generation in the *New England Journal of Science*. The paper was published by Professor Stanislaw McCloud. I recognized my equations. In a few months' time, a man who had been scorned by the world of academic research suddenly became a celebrity. Reporters besieged the M.I.T. campus. The *Washington Post* heralded Professor McCloud as 'The Next Einstein.'

"Funds from the Federal government and foundations flooded the Physics department to build the first particle accelerator at M.I.T. What Professor McCloud didn't know was that I had painstakingly copied my equations in long hand on several exercise books which I still kept. By some error, while I was transferring the formulae and equations to the mainframe, I had skipped ten pages of equations in the fifth exercise book. After studying Professor McCloud's equations more closely, a group of scientists attacked his findings and exposed the equations to be a scientific hoax. They tore his paper apart, criticized the limitations of his equations, and denounced him as a charlatan. To cut a long story short, McCloud was removed as head of the scientific research team at M.I.T. A year later he lost his post as chair of the department. He had lost all scientific credibility and soon became a laughingstock in academic circles. I transferred to UCLA where I was allowed to retain my course work and comprehensive exam results. In less than four years, I completed a PhD in Pure Physics. I left for home immediately, after graduation, when I obtained my diploma."

It was an amazing narrative. My gaze was riveted on Matanda's face throughout the narration of this remarkable experience in the U.S. "What happened when you got home?" I heard myself ask him.

"I was immediately recruited in the Ministry of Scientific Research. The first desktops had just been produced. I began reconstituting my equations in my office in the Ministry with an Apple computer I brought from the U.S. After I had been in the Ministry for three years I met the minister and explained the potential of my scientific data. He was excited. He was happy that I had not opted to stay abroad. He was a Beti man, with a PhD in Anthropology. He handed my proposal of building a particle accelerator in our country to the technical adviser of the ministry who happened to be a French expatriate. The technical adviser convinced the minister that I was too ambitious and could be mentally unbalanced. The kind of research I was proposing, the French man told the minister, could not be realized in a developing country. A year later the minister was removed from his post in an unexpected cabinet reshuffle. A new man replaced him. The French technical adviser still maintained his post. I tried to see the new minister but could not. Six months later I offered my resignation and left the ministry."

"And what about FIST, the opposition political party? What's the relationship between the party and your Institute?"

"None, whatsoever. The initials that make up the acronyms of the party and my Institute are a sheer coincidence. I don't know Jani Frandi. We've never met. I'm not interested in politics, Mr Fondo. I hope my story answers your questions."

"You know I'm a journalist. You didn't bring me here to reveal the nature of your research to the world, did you?"

"Certainly not."

"Dr Matanda, I'll like to know why you brought me here."

"I'll let you know, Mr Fondo. As soon as we finish the tour of the premises, I'll take you to the lab complex where I conduct my most crucial experiments. It's at the complex that you'll find out why I brought you here."

"Before I forget, Dr Matanda, let me confess that I'm impressed by the variety of natural foods you offered for breakfast. What about the strawberries? Where do they come from, if I may ask?"

"Everything we eat in the Institute is home-grown, all year round. And all of it is organic. There's an orchard beyond the hills near the laboratories in which we grow fruits."

"And what about drinking water?"

"There're lots of springs in the estate. I constructed an irrigation system ten years ago that feeds the orchard and vegetable farms. Fast running mountain streams facilitated the generation of electricity from small turbines in five micro-hydro plants linked by a grid system."

"From what you say, the Institute is self-sufficient."

"It is. I had no other choice. To do what I'm doing here, I had to operate in complete seclusion from the outside world. I hope you liked the food."

"It was wonderful. The muffins and fruit juices in particular."

"Good." Dr Matanda looked at his watch. "We can have more of the fruit juices later on in the day."

I stood up. "This has been the best breakfast I've had in years."

"I'll let Kuma Tah know. He'll be flattered. Can we begin the tour?"

5

We started the tour from Matanda's main house which he nostalgically referred to as 'the central living quarters.' We left the dining room and walked down a flight of stairs to a corridor from which one door led to the kitchen and the other to Matanda's living room, study, and bedroom. It was a small bungalow with limited but functional space. Matanda said it made sense to have a small house since he lived alone. Next to the main house were two buildings, 'the other living quarters,' that housed Kuma Tah, the technicians, bodyguard, and driver. He pointed to the guest quarters where I had spent the night, explaining that they could accommodate as many as twenty guests a time without too much inconvenience. We walked for about ten minutes, going up a gentle slope on top of which was situated the main laboratory complex. I noticed a small building with a chimney to my left as we ascended the hill. I pointed at the house and commented that it looked secluded. Matanda barely glanced at the building. He simply said the house was a crematorium. Another road continued behind the lab complex into the distance ahead of us. I asked Matanda where the road went to.

"The road goes to the food and vegetable sections. The orchard is about half a mile away from the food and vegetable vicinity. One weekend is not enough for you to see the entire

Institute. Look at that cliff beyond the small hills over there," he said, pointing at a distant precipice. "Can you see it?"

"Yes. The one with the cloud over it."

"The road behind the lab complex goes past the vegetable and orchard sections to that cliff. A small electrical locomotive is located where the paved road ends and continues half a kilometre into a tunnel inside the cliff where a vertical elevator shaft descends fifty meters deep into the ground. That's where the particle accelerator is located. Two technicians work with the accelerator; they also assist me with the experiments in the lab complex."

We entered the lab complex through the main door and walked down a small hallway. In front of us I saw a structure that defied description. It seemed to be a separate building within the complex. I noticed that its roof had a dome-like, concave shape. When we got to the structure, Matanda opened a door and we went up a flight of stairs. We alighted onto a small rectangular room with several electronic controls and a big, flat, LCD screen. Two men sat on high revolving chairs. They were busy adjusting and manipulating several instruments on an illuminated electronic console. They both wore earphones and microphones. They worked methodically with professional dexterity, born out of experience. They paid no attention to us as we entered the room. I noticed two extra chairs in the control room.

Dr Matanda said, "This is the central control room from which we monitor what goes on in the vacuum chamber. These men are the technicians I mentioned. They have a spare chair reserved for you. They're getting the chamber ready for a man and a woman who are expected to pass through it this afternoon."

"You mean you have other guests in the Institute? I would like to meet them."

"You'll see them, but you won't meet them," Dr Matanda said brusquely. "Guests in the Institute are forbidden to meet each other. They come here separately and depart separately. We're about to enter the antechamber. Give us a view of the rooms," Dr Matanda said to one of the technicians.

"Yes, sir," the man said. He pressed a button in front of him and the closed-circuit screen came on. He pressed a second button and the images of three rooms began alternating, one after the other, on the screen. I came closer to the screen and scrutinized the images.

"As you can see," Dr Matanda said, "several cameras have been mounted in the anteroom and vacuum chamber to provide us with multiple views in the control room and to enable us monitor the subject as the experiment progresses. However, it's only the antechamber that has an intercom.

"You see, I had always been intrigued by the connection between the human mind, matter, and the human imagination. I was convinced the three were interrelated, and that mind can control matter. Imagination is God's greatest gift to man and woman. Imagination unites humanity with God. The human imagination, like God, can create non-existing realities or alter existing ones, if it so desires. With imagination, a people can dream, have visions, and create their desired realities. What will the future hold for mankind if humans were stripped of their potential to imagine?" Dr Matanda asked me.

"It will be bleak," I answered. "Perhaps this is what's wrong with our country. How could God bestow mankind with imagination, but our people seem not to utilize it?" I asked

Dr Matanda. "Are we different from the rest of humanity?"

"The vast majority of people in this country appear to have no imagination," Dr Matanda went on.

"I think they do," I said. "Maybe it lies dormant, somewhere inside them."

"Of what use is an endowment if its recipient is unaware of it. If, as you say, the gift of imagination is hidden in the individual's mind, how useful is that individual to humanity? Anyone without imagination has no purpose for existence. They might as well be dead. This is why I constructed the vacuum chamber: to enable me identify people with imagination. The membrane of the last door in the vacuum chamber can only be transcended with a concentrated mind and a finely tuned imagination. Unfortunately, the vast majority of people do not succeed to go through the chamber."

"What happens to them? I mean to those who do not succeed to pass through the chamber."

"I abhor seeing what happens to them; but the chamber was designed to do just that—suffocate them to death because they did not manifest God's mind."

"Where do these people come from—the subjects for your experiments?"

"From all over the country. Both men and women come here. It's interesting to note that women perform better than men. I've come to conclude that women are more imaginative than men. Many people have heard of the Institute. I have recruiting agents in the ten regions. Most of the participants in my experiments get in touch with recruiting agents who are spread all over the country. No one comes here against his or her will. Your case is different though. It's the exception rather the rule."

"What do you do with the corpses of those who don't go through the chamber?" I asked Dr Matanda.

"I get rid of them in the crematorium you saw on our way here. They simply disappear."

I thought about what he had just said. I felt a cold shiver run down my spine. I wondered whether Dr Matanda had lost his sanity. "Have you weighed the ethical choice of good and evil in what you're doing?" I asked him. "You're responsible for the deaths of so many people," I said with dismay.

A short smile appeared on his face. "That's a mistaken view," he said. "I don't kill anyone, Mr Fondo. Most of them are dead before they arrive here. I merely dispose of their bodies."

"What happens to subjects who change their minds after they get here?" I asked him.

"I explain to them what I'm doing as soon as they get to the Institute. If they're unwilling to participate in the experiments, I administer them a memory alteration drug that wipes off any recollection of their having come here, just before I drop them from where I picked them up."

"So the two guests you mentioned came here on their own volition."

"I'd like to think so. As I said, you'll have a chance to see them go through the chamber. Then you'll make up your mind to do the same thing. That's why I brought you here."

"And if I refuse."

"It will be unfortunate indeed, Mr Fondo. My inquiries about you suggest you possess an astonishing imagination. However, if you decline, I'll have no other choice than to take you back from where we picked you up."

I reflected for a moment. "We'll see," I said, "we'll see

what happens."

"Come on," Dr Matanda said, "I'd like to take you to the meditation room."

We left the control room via a wooden door and entered a short lobby that was connected to two doors. The wooden door on the left was closed. The other door in front of us was constructed of aluminium. The door had no visible handle or lock. Matanda pressed a red button to the left of the door. Seconds later, the door slid open to the left with a soft hydraulic hiss. We stepped into a room and the door slid shut with another hiss. It was a small room of about four by five metres with a low ceiling and subdued lighting. The room had a single chair. Another metallic door, much like the first one, was on the opposite wall in front of us.

"This antechamber serves as a meditation room. Can you hear me?" Dr Matanda asked. A synthesized metallic voice said, "Yes, sir, loud and clear."

"We installed an intercom between the control room and the meditation room," Dr Matanda carried on, "because there were numerous instances when subjects declined to enter the vacuum chamber at the last minute. If and when your turn comes, you'll be left alone here to meditate and focus your thoughts on the task ahead of you."

"And what exactly is this task?" I asked Dr Matanda.

"To open the seven doors in the next room. Each door is actually part of a small rectangular cubicle. The vacuum chamber is, in fact, two rooms constructed entirely of pure steel. The first of the two rooms is the larger and longer one. and this door in front of us leads into this room."

"This makes seven small cubicles then in this first part of the chamber."

"You're right," Dr Matanda said. "You can also call it 'the room of mirrors'. The seven doors are composed of interconnecting mirrors that can only be opened with the mind and imagination. Sensors on the locks pick up one's thought impressions and register them as electromagnetic energy units that in turn trigger the hydraulic lock of each door to open. The concentration of one's mind and mental impressions must be focused on just one single thought—to prime open the seven locks. As soon as the seven doors open, this triggers the mechanism that opens the next door leading into the second and last section of the chamber. This section of the chamber is a total vacuum. The room has no air, no oxygen. The last door in this room is made up of a special translucent membrane composed of fibre glass, reinforced plastic, and other materials. One can only last in this chamber as long as the last inhaled breath can sustain him or her. The translucent door is the only escape outlet. The door has a lock but no key. Like the doors in the preceding chamber, it's fitted with sensors that pick up mind impressions and register them as electromagnetic energy units that will release the lock. You must unite mind impressions, imagination, and will power to open this last door."

"If I understand you well, Dr Matanda, since the door leading into the vacuum chamber is a one-way door, one can't go back to the preceding room. If you can't penetrate the membrane while your breath lasts, then it's certain you will die."

"Exactly. The vacuum chamber is a one-way journey to self-liberation or a certain death."

"Female subject is just about ready, sir," I heard the synthesized voice of one of the technicians announce over the intercom.

"Give us five minutes," Dr Matanda responded. "Let's go back to the control room and watch the first subject." He pressed a red button in the room much like the one outside and the door slid open. It closed as soon as we stepped out of the room. We crossed the short hallway and went up the control room. Matanda asked me to sit down. He pulled the other chair and sat down; then he took a third pair of headphones with a microphone and wore them on his head.

"Okay," Dr Matanda said," "we're about to begin, Mr Fondo. I advise you to keep your attention on the flat screen and follow the procedure with us."

"Proceed with female subject to anteroom," the second technician spoke quietly in his microphone.

A minute or so passed and I saw a woman come into view on the flat screen and enter the meditation room. The image on the screen was in full colour. The woman was dark and tall, with long slender fingers and angular facial features. She wore a matching wrapper suit and headscarf. I saw her sit on the chair.

"How many minutes would you want for meditation, Madam?" Dr Matanda asked her, speaking quietly into a microphone.

"Ten minutes will be sufficient," the woman's synthesized voice responded over the intercom.

We all stayed quiet in the control room. My eyes were glued on the flat screen. The woman kept very still. From time to time, I glanced at my watch. Matanda kept on looking at the wall clock in front of him.

"It's now ten minutes," Dr Matanda told the woman. "Proceed to the first part of the chamber."

The woman stood up and walked to the door in front of her. She pressed the red button with her left hand and the door slid open. The door slid shut behind her as she walked into the other room. Cameras in the next room focused on her as she entered the room. The picture on the flat screen alternated to a bigger picture of her face that filled the entire screen. Her eyes were closed. I saw her lips move rapidly. I couldn't say whether she was talking to herself or muttering a silent prayer. After a while, her lips stopped moving, but her eyes stayed closed for two or three additional minutes. She opened her eyes and looked intently at the lock in front of her. Her gaze was steadfast, focused. I looked at my watch. Time slipped by. Ten minutes were now gone. Eleven, twelve. The woman's gaze was still concentrated on the door. Thirteen minutes. That was when the door slid open, revealing the other seven doors. They were all wide open. Another camera focused again on the woman as she walked through the seven doors.

She seemed to take a deep breath before she stepped into the vacuum chamber. She walked quickly across the room and stood in front of the translucent door. I wondered how long she could stay like that without air. It was getting to twenty seconds when I saw her stretch her right hand slowly and put her palm in front of the translucent door. Moments later the translucent membrane began to pulsate and glow in a pale blue light. I saw the soft, blue glow on the membrane expand and slowly envelope her outstretched hand. Almost immediately, in a flash, the door slid open. She stepped out of the chamber and, in an instant, the door slid shut. She had not spent up to thirty seconds in the vacuum chamber. The two technicians looked at each other. The first man switched

off the intercom and removed the headphones and microphone from his head. Dr Matanda and the second technician
removed their headphones. I breathed a sigh of relief.

Matanda simply said, "Excellent."

I did not know what to make of the whole thing. Had the
woman really made any mental effort to open the hydraulic
doors or had Dr Matanda and his technical crew actually con-
trolled the doors to open after an agreed time and sequence
of events? Was I watching a mechanical pantomime in which
Dr Matanda was directing and stage-managing the whole
show? Where did reality begin and illusion end?

"Where's the woman now?" I asked Dr Matanda. "What
has happened to her?"

"She's alive and well, but exhausted and depleted of
mental energy. She has been taken to the recuperating room
for a brief period of rest before Jean-Bosco and Lipenja take
her back to the guest quarters."

"What about the man you mentioned? When will his
turn come?" I asked Dr Matanda.

He looked at the clock on the wall. "In another twenty
minutes. Some air has entered the vacuum chamber. It will
take about fifteen minutes to extract it from the room and
restore it to full vacuum capacity. Lipenja and Jean-Bosco
will let us know."

It didn't take up to twenty minutes when a man came into
view on the flat screen as he entered the antechamber. "Okay,"
Dr Matanda said, as he looked at the clock, "the chamber has
been restored to full vacuum capacity. Male subject is now
seated in meditation room. Switch on the intercom and put
on your headgears." The first technician pushed a button as
he activated the intercom. They all put on their headphones

and microphones.

"Can you hear me?" Dr Matanda asked the man in the meditation room.

"Yes sir. Loud and clear," the man's voice responded over the intercom. He sounded unsure, unconvinced. "I'm ready."

"Good," Dr Matanda said. "How many minutes would you require for meditation."

"Twenty," the man's voice replied back.

"Twenty minutes then," Dr Matanda assured him. "Take your time."

Twenty minutes later the man stood up. He walked towards the door leading into the room of mirrors and pressed the red button. The door slid shut behind him as he stepped into the other room. His face came into full focus on the flat screen. I seemed to detect a trace of lethargy and absentmindedness on the features of the enlarged face. He stayed in the room for close to twenty-five minutes as he concentrated on the seven locks. His face became rigid as time passed. I stole a quick glance at Matanda. He seemed unworried. Twenty-six minutes later the seven locks sprang open and the man walked through them, one after the other. Another camera focused on his countenance and projected his bloated face on the monitor in the control room. I could see beads of perspiration on his face as he walked across the vacuum chamber. I saw him close his eyes as he focused his mind on the last door. His face looked weary as if he had used up all his mental energy in the room of mirrors. There was evident panic on his face when he opened his eyes. Even before he stretched his right hand at the translucent membrane, I knew he would not make it. All of a sudden, we watched him clutch his chest and collapse on the floor. I watched helplessly as his body convulsed on the floor in his desperate search for air to breathe. I turned my eyes away from the screen. It was too distressing to watch a man die in such utter agony.

"It's all over for him," Dr Matanda said sadly. "That's it for this afternoon. It's close to lunch time. Lipenja and Jean-Bosco will remove his remains from the chamber and carry them to the crematorium." He turned away from the technicians and looked at me. "If you think you're up to it, let me know."

"My mind's already made up," I said. "I'm ready."

"Splendid!" Dr Matanda said. "Let's give ourselves a few hours of rest after lunch then we'll come back here and it will be your turn."

"That's fine with me."

Matanda removed his microphone and headphones. The first technician switched off the intercom. Matanda and I came out of the lab complex and walked back to the living quarters for lunch.

6

After a brief siesta, we returned to the lab complex at 4 PM. Lipenja, Matanda, and I stood in the lobby for a few minutes before we dispersed.

"I'll leave you now and join the technicians in the control room," Dr Matanda said. "Lipenja will escort you to the antechamber. From there on, you're on your own. You have enough time in the antechamber to let me know if you—"

"My mind's already made up. I won't change it." I unfastened my watch from my left wrist and handed it to Matanda. "It will be a distraction. I'll pick it up when I'm through." Matanda wished me good luck as he left us and walked down the lobby.

"This way, sir," Lipenja said. "Please follow me."

I walked with Lipenja in the direction of the control room. We made a right turn and walked down another corridor that came to an end in front of a wooden door. Lipenja opened the door and I found myself in the short lobby from the control room. Lipenja pointed at the automatic door. "Here you are, sir. This is the door into the meditation room. The red button there opens the door. Good luck."

The door hissed open as I pressed the red button and stepped into the antechamber. I walked across the room and sat down on the chair. I knew Matanda and the technicians were observing me on the flat screen.

"How many minutes do you want for contemplation?" I heard Dr Matanda's crisp voice ask over the intercom.

"Five minutes."

"Five minutes will be fine," Dr Matanda answered back.

I closed my eyes, took in several deep breaths and tried to relax my mind. I visualized myself in the room of mirrors. It did not take long for the first door to appear. My eyes were still closed. I tried to bring the door into focus. All of a sudden, I found myself in the room in front of the first door. I accepted this visualization as reality. I concentrated again on the seven locks, in a relaxed manner, without straining the mind. This time I heard the seven locks click open.

"Your five minutes are over," Dr Matanda's synthesized voice in the intercom interrupted my visualization. "Time to go," I heard him say.

I opened my eyes. I was elated but calm as I stood up and walked towards the second automatic door. I pressed the red button and the door slid open to the left with a soft hiss. I stepped into the room of mirrors and the door shut back with another hiss. There was no going back now. I saw the first door and its mirrors in front of me. I knew there were seven of them and I had adequate time to concentrate on opening the locks and filling my lungs with enough air before stepping into the vacuum chamber. I concentrated on the locks as I banished all other thoughts from my mind. *The locks. Open the locks. Just the locks, nothing else. Let them open.* Open. Open. I heard the connecting click of several locks opening at the same time and a soft collective metallic hiss. Almost at once I saw the seven doors slide open in front of me.

I stepped forward and walked through them in a casual,

unhurried pace. I felt myself breathing deeply. I took in one huge gulp of air before I stepped into the vacuum chamber. The hydraulic door hissed shut behind me. I *have to hold my breath*, I reminded myself. *This room has no air*. I had trained myself to hold my breath for two minutes. I wondered how my system would cope without air beyond two minutes. The translucent door was about five meters away from me, I estimated, as I crossed the room in quick rapid strides. I came up to the door and stood in front of it. I closed my eyes and imagined myself standing outside the door on the other side. I felt the seconds ticking away. Half a minute must have gone by. I opened my eyes and looked at the door. It was still closed.

I closed my eyes again and focused my mind on the door. A long time passed, but I heard no hissing sound. I felt the seconds ticking away. I had just about twenty seconds of airtime left. My lungs were now yearning for air. Ten more seconds. I lifted my right hand and pointed at the translucent membrane with my palm. Nothing happened! It felt like eternity. I knew my lungs had reached their maximum capacity of two minutes. I was now stretching them into extra time. Why had the door not opened? What had happened to my mind and its capacity to imagine? What had happened to my imagination? I needed air now. I had to start breathing again. Then something clicked inside me. I was trying too hard. All of a sudden, I let myself go. Air or nor air, I didn't care any longer. I ceased to struggle against the moment. Whether I lived or died did not matter anymore to me. If I was about to die, I would die without a struggle.

I felt my consciousness receding from my body. It was a floating sensation, as if my feet had left the floor. Almost at once, I felt my face and lungs flooded with much-needed air. My eyes were still closed. When I opened them, I was no longer in the vacuum chamber! I was outside! Till this day, I wonder whether it wasn't a trick played on my mind by Dr Matanda, his technicians, and his strange instruments. But there I was, in a small corridor inside the laboratory complex. I felt dizzy as if I had fallen from a great height. Then I blacked out.

It was Matanda's face I saw when I opened my eyes. "Congratulations! It was extraordinary!" There was a trace of excitement in his voice. I was on a bed, in a small white room with no windows. I transferred my feet from the bed onto the floor. I still had my shoes on.

"Where am I?" I asked Dr Matanda. "What happened?"

"You passed out momentarily, Mr Fondo," Matanda said. "Nothing serious. A little bit of fatigue, I'm sure. We brought you here to rest. This is a minor surgical room that doubles as a recuperating room. You made it, Mr Fondo!"

I looked around the room. Apart from one computer on a small office desk, a filing cabinet, a microscope, and what appeared to be a high intensity movable light, there was nothing else in the room. I saw Matanda peel off a pair of surgical gloves he was wearing and throw them into a trash can. The second technician was holding a liver-shaped dish in his hand. He walked out with it when my feet touched the floor. Apart from a sore feeling on the back of my neck, I felt fine. I looked at Matanda as I stood up from the bed. I noticed that he was wearing a white lab coat.

"How long was I out?"

"Oh, not more than five minutes. How do you feel?"

"A little bit unsteady, but okay, I guess."

"Here, have your watch. Let's go down to the living quarters. You need an extended rest."

I took my watch and strapped it on my wrist. Matanda removed the lab coat he wore and placed it on top of the computer table. We came out of the room, walked down a familiar corridor and left the complex through the main entrance. I walked down unsteadily with Matanda to the living quarters. He told me to rest for about thirty minutes and that supper will be ready in about an hour.

I went to my room, lay down on the bed and closed my eyes. I did not know when I fell asleep. It was Jean-Bosco's voice that woke me up. "You're late for supper, Mr Fondo," I heard Jean-Bosco shouting and banging the door.

"Okay, I heard you. I'll be there in ten minutes." I glanced at my watch. It was a quarter to eight. I had slept for more than one hour. I got out of bed, washed my face and brushed my teeth. I came out of my room and walked over to Matanda's main building. I apologized for having overslept.

Matanda waved aside my apology. "It was a well-deserved rest," he reassured me. "The food is still warm. Kuma Tah brought it from the kitchen just five minutes ago. It's a light supper of crepes and lemon grass tea."

I sat down and we began to eat. In between mouthfuls I asked Matanda about my performance.

"We've never seen anything like this before. I mean the technicians and myself. It was unprecedented. You didn't just pass through the door, you also levitated. We have it all on tape. A few seconds after your palm was pointed at the translucent door, a strange thing happened. The magnetic resonance of your vibrations exceeded what we normally see. Your entire body was surrounded by an aura of blue light so bright that it hurt our eyes seeing it on the screen. And then your feet left the floor! The sensors were supposed to slide the door open. This did not happen. Instead you disappeared from the chamber! You hesitated momentarily, half a meter from the floor and literally vanished through the door. Remarkable, Mr Fondo! This has never happened before. We could not believe our eyes! Theoretically the anti-gravity effect exists in my formulae and equations as a possibility. But this … this vanishing from the vacuum chamber and transcending the material composition of the translucent door—this defies scientific rationalization. The powers of your mind and imagination must be astounding for this effect to really happen. There must be something very spiritual or saintly about you, Mr Fondo."

"I don't know, Dr Matanda. I still think it's some kind of illusion you're playing with my mind. One moment I felt trapped in the chamber, and the next moment I found myself outside. It defies anything rational."

"But it happened, Mr Fondo! You experienced it yourself. How do you explain it?"

"I don't know."

"Would you like to see the dead man? He's not yet been cremated."

"That will not be necessary. I'm convinced he really died. I saw him die."

When supper was over, I bade Matanda goodnight before we separated. He reminded me that breakfast the next morning will be at six, so I had to get up quite early. I thanked him for the evening and went back to my room for a long night's rest.

7

I changed into my own clothes on Sunday morning before I joined Matanda for breakfast at six. My shirt, trousers, inner wear, and jacket had been washed and ironed. Jean-Bosco was already revving the car when I got to the garage at six thirty. Matanda and I got into the back seat of the car. The driver brought the car out and drove slowly up the hill that led to the mountains. We drove for a while in silence.

"What do you think was wrong with the man who could not go through the vacuum chamber?" I asked Dr Matanda? "At least he succeeded in opening the locks in the first section of the chamber, didn't he?"

"He did," Dr Matanda agreed. "But he seemed to lack a sense of purpose."

"I thought he was absentminded too," I added.

"You may be right," Dr Matanda said. "He spent too much time in the meditation room and stayed much longer in the room of mirrors. Unfortunately, there wasn't much creative imagination left in him by the time he reached the vacuum chamber itself."

"With all these fascinating ideas you have and the experiments you're conducting, you should be with the people, living with them. You could start a movement and there would be change in this country. Isolating yourself in these mountains does not help liberate our people from their fettered minds."

"I have thought about it all these years," Dr Matanda said, after reflecting for a while, "but I rejected that option. Old habits die hard. I would be taken for a mad man. My wasted years in the Ministry are proof of it. I've often wondered how I maintained my sanity in that place. That's why I opted to conduct my experiments in the isolation of these mountains.

"Every time I venture out of the Institute, I am overwhelmed by the anarchy and chaos in which our people live. Let me give you one or two banal examples. The regime in power has no think tank that can formulate and shape policy in anticipation of the future. What will our population be in eighty or a hundred years to come? How will our city streets and highways cope with this increase in population? How shall we manage our urban waste? Take our capital city for example. Look at the traffic jams, the accumulated garbage in the streets, the gaping potholes. Pavements which were meant for families to stroll on have been swamped by street hawkers, garages, broken down cars, markets. Truck pushers with planks jostle in the same narrow streets with motorbikes, dilapidated taxi cabs, stray dogs, and fruit vendors. Motorists throw sugarcane, orange, groundnuts, and banana peelings into the streets as they drive by. Men and women urinate in casual abandon everywhere on street corners—. Stop! Stop the car!" Dr Matanda yelled at the driver.

Jean-Bosco stepped on the brakes and the car came to a hasty halt. I did not have my seatbelt on and was catapulted against the back of the driver's seat. I regained my balance and hastily strapped on my seatbelt. Matanda's hands were trembling and he was sweating profusely. His breathing was strained. I thought he was having a heart attack. I reached out with my right hand and tried to touch him.

"Don't!" he said, waving off my extended hand. He brought out a handkerchief from his pocket and covered his mouth. After a while, he closed his mouth and wiped his perspiring face with the handkerchief. "I almost threw up. This is what happens every time my mind gets into the filth and anarchy of this country, six decades after independence. It always makes me sick."

"And yet we had so much potential," I carried on, talking more to myself than to him.

"Yes," he said. "As much potential as Thailand, Indonesia, or Malaysia. Look at where we are today. We don't have much to show to the world, have we?"

"Come on," I said, "we do. Beer in all its varieties, hip-wriggling *Bikutsi*[2] rhythms. At least these have taken the world by storm!"

He managed a muted chuckle that seemed to relieve his tension. "You have a wry sense of humour, Mr Fondo. Yes, beer and football. Come to think of it, you could be right. They keep the people's minds distracted from their predicament. How funny! I'm all right now Jean-Bosco. We can continue."

Jean-Bosco started the car. We drove down for another fifteen minutes before the car came to a gentle stop. It was the same spot the car had stopped when we come up the mountain road on Friday.

"We'll come out here," Dr Matanda said. "I want to show you something. You remember this place, don't you?"

[2] A kind of dance.

Jean-Bosco, Matanda, and I came out of the car.

"Yes, I do. This is where you said we could not drive through, although I clearly saw a road in front of us." Jean-Bosco opened the trunk and came back with the metallic briefcase. He handed it to Matanda.

"And now, a little demonstration," Dr Matanda announced. "Please step in front of the car, raise your hands and stretch them out in front of you. Walk slowly. Very slowly."

I moved in front of the car and raised my hands up, palms facing outwards. I began walking forward slowly. "There's nothing," I said, glancing briefly at him, "except the road in front of me."

"A few more steps," Dr Matanda said. "You will feel it."

"Feel what?" I took three steps and was about to say something when my outstretched hands felt a solid object. I withdrew my hands at once and lowered them. I was frightened. "What's going on here? I touched something! My hands have come up against an unseen, invisible barrier!"

"That's the force field. Don't be afraid. It's actually a band of energy vibrating at a regulated frequency. It's much like the wind. You can feel it, but you can't see it. It won't harm you, Mr Fondo. Go on, raise your hands and feel it again," Matanda urged me.

I raised my hands slowly and felt the barrier. I pushed hard against it with all my strength. I moved my hands sideways, up and down. There was something preventing me from going forward. I put down my hands and kicked the space in front of me with my right foot. I grabbed my foot instantly and skipped back to the car. It hurt so badly.

"You've got to be careful," Dr Matanda cautioned me "The thing is as solid as a rock. Now, while you're massaging your sore foot, let's see what we can do." He placed the electronic box on the car, opened it, and fiddled around with the dials and switches. I felt that strange pulsating sound again. Like the other day, it went on for five minutes. Then I saw a burst of white light in the sky. When the vibrations died down, Matanda said, "Now stretch your hands forward again."

I raised both hands and pushed hard, expecting the same resistance. I lost my balance and almost fell down. "Good God!" I cried out. "It's gone! It's no longer there!" For lack of words, I said, "It's just air! Empty air! Incredible!" I muttered, as I turned round and faced Matanda. "Unbelievable! How does this work?"

"The principle is quite simple. The particle accelerator I built in the mountain speeds up photons and collides them, creating tremendous energy. I've managed to harness this energy into a force field. What I needed was a system to control it. It took me another three years to invent this electronic box. As you must have noticed, the force field is activated and deactivated by the box. I call it the black box because of the colour of the briefcase."

"Remarkable! Absolutely incredible!"

"This is the kind of scientific research I tried to convince the Ministry about when I was there. Our oil wells will eventually dry out. Prices of cocoa and coffee have plummeted in the world markets. There is advanced research in the West to develop synthetic cocoa and coffee. This force field technology would be the gateway for an alternative source of income for this country. Industrialized nations would beat a path to our doorsteps.

"We could sell this technology to Western powers who are nuts about military defence. And they would pay whatever price our government demanded. With the huge profits we would make, we would jumpstart our development and eventually catch up with South Eastern Asia and the rest of the world. This was my vision. But no one would listen to me. The French technical adviser convinced the minister that my PhD in what he termed 'abstractions into the world of subatomic particles,' had unhinged my mind."

"You're a genius, Dr Matanda."

The features of his oval face relaxed into a broad smile. "Thank you," he said. "Thank you very much, Mr Fondo." He closed the briefcase and gave it to Jean-Bosco. He glanced at his watch and said, "It's getting to seven. Let's get going. There's just one bush taxi that comes to Mbekakum. It leaves around nine o'clock. We still have about ten minutes before we get to the boulder barrier."

Ten minutes later we reached the two boulders. The huge rocks blocked the small narrow road. This time I wasn't surprised. The driver pressed several black and red knobs on the gadget mounted on the dashboard. I felt the same tremor and vibrations I had perceived the first day. As soon as the tremor subsided, the two boulders parted to reveal the road in front of us. Jean-Bosco eased the car slowly past the narrow opening.

"This was the first security system I installed to prevent unwanted people from trespassing into the Institute," Dr Matanda said. "It took me several more years before I perfected the force field. The rocks close back five minutes after the car passes through the narrow entrance."

As we descended the narrow mountain road to Mbekakum, Matanda filled me with amusing details about the force field. Apparently, the villagers had come to associate the

mountains with witchcraft. The occasional burst of mysterious lights in the sky and the discovery of dead birds that
had collided against the invisible field kept the villagers away
from the mysterious mountains.

"Oh!" he added, "I forgot telling you. You've been assigned
an SIN, a Serial Identification Number, a unit, and a section."

"What's that supposed to mean?" I asked him, a hint of
suspicion settling on my face.

"Everyone who goes through the vacuum chamber is
tagged electronically and registered in the database of a central computer."

"You mean you've tagged me?"

"Send your left hand behind your neck," Dr Matanda said.
"I unbuttoned two of my shirt buttons and did as he said.
I felt a small scratch, much like a tiny blister on my neck.

"When did you do it?" I asked him. "How did you do it?"

"The tag is beneath the skin. It's too tiny to be seen or felt.
It's a hundred times thinner than the human hair. I used a
microscope to implant it underneath your skin. We carried
out the procedure in the recuperating room while you rested.
In two days' time, the blister will disappear."

"You didn't tell me," I protested.

"I didn't have to. I usually don't reveal this information
to other people. They leave the Institute without knowing
they've been tagged. Because you're a journalist you need
to know the truth—"

"The whole truth," I cut in.

"And nothing but the truth," Dr Matanda added with a
grin.

"And what's my serial number?"

"XG467PJ878, Unit 5, Section 10."

"How many of us are out there? How many of us have graduated from the Institute?"

"Many more than you can imagine. I need to reach a particular number that will constitute the critical mass to begin the revolution that will change this country."

"And what number will achieve this critical mass?"

"That's information I can't release to you."

"Well, how many more people do you have to tag before you reach this critical mass?"

"A few more thousands. The identification rate is terribly slow. My statistics indicate a failure rate of two hundred and fifty to five. Probably in fifteen or twenty more years from now, I'll attain the critical mass. The central computer will then activate the electronic tags embedded in all of you and send a transmission to your minds."

"What happens after that?"

"A new way of thinking will begin," Dr Matanda said. His face seemed to glow in illumination. "Beyond that I can't say precisely what direction the nation will go. The change will be for the better. For that I'm quite certain. That's the moment I've been waiting for all these years, when I'll leave these mountains and settle among the people."

"You want to be some kind of leader? Do you see yourself leading the people?"

"Perhaps," Dr Matanda replied reflectively. "I don't know for sure. It will be up to the people to decide for themselves."

I found myself wondering about this kind of upheaval that Matanda visualized. "The status quo, the regime in power," I said, "will resist the change. The revolution you envisage will be bloody."

"So be it," Dr Matanda responded grimly. "That will be

the price we'll pay for a better tomorrow."

We got to the outskirts of Mbekakum at eight thirty. I heard a cock crow and a dog barking in the distance. Spirals of blue smoke rose lazily from a number of huts on the hillsides. The driver manoeuvred the car to a small junction, turned it round and let it face the direction from which we had come. I came out of the car and looked around. Matanda too came out.

"It's been a delight knowing that you really exist, Dr Matanda," I said as I shook hands with him.

"The pleasure has been mine, Mr Fondo. Keep your imagination alive. I count on you in the not-too-distant future."

"Now that you really exist in flesh and blood," I told Dr Matanda, "I wonder how I can embody you in my weekly column."

Matanda reflected for a while and said "A short story of course! Write a story about a mysterious house of mirrors in some remote mountain. It will fascinate your readers."

"You think they will believe it?"

"Well," he said. "You never can tell. I'll leave you here. It will take you about five minutes to walk down to the small village square where a bush taxi leaves at around nine. The taxi takes approximately one and a half hours to reach Mendankwe. There're a lot of motorbikes that run between Mendankwe and Bamenda. You should get to Yaoundé before five in the evening."

There were only two more people left to fill the bush taxi when I got to the village square. In just under five minutes the taxi was full. The driver revved the engine and hooted twice before the taxi lurched forward and began the slow descent from Mbekakum. The strategic seat I occupied by a window gave me a vantage position to observe the rugged terrain and vista of the undulating mountains. I looked at my watch. It was nine fifteen. We had not gone far when a dense fog began rolling down the mountains. The taxi made a sharp bend to the left and I glanced up to look at the mountains. They had disappeared—completely swallowed up by the descending fog. It was as if the mountains never existed.

A Handful of Earth

If it were not of Bridget Bijanga, the antagonism between Veke Lucasi and Saddi Tegene would have remained uneventful. It would have, probably, fizzled out after both boys graduated from Bonjongo Catholic elementary school. Bijanga knew that Lucasi and Saddi admired her, but she did not know that her attraction to both boys would lead to their eventual self-destruction. Bijanga was the school belle. Fair in complexion with elongated limbs and small delicate fingers, she was endowed with full-blossomed cheeks, sensuous lips, thick bushy eyebrows, and large eyes, all set on a narrow forehead. She was one of only five girls in Class Five who had developed breasts. Her breasts were small and cone-shaped. Whenever she smiled, she stunned the boys with her two symmetrical rows of gleaming ivory-white teeth. Her smile was disarming, invitingly provocative.

There was something peculiarly distinctive in her family name. Perhaps it was the unique and unusual arrangement of vowels and consonants that coalesced to form the name Bijanga. No one could say. Her first name, Bridget, was soon forgotten after her third year in the school. It was at the end of the third term, when Class Four children attended their first music lesson in preparation of discovering those with good voices before the long holidays. Auntie Nams, the music teacher, was the one who first said Bridget sounded foreign and un-African. She said she preferred Bijanga because it sounded melodious. After that music lesson the whole school, including her teachers, began calling her Bijanga.

Nicknamed 'Son of Lucifer' by his classmates, Lucasi was one among a handful of boys in the school who knew how to order charms, perfumes, and rings from India. He was actually the first boy in the school to order a magic ring. He also possessed the legendry Six and Seven flowers perfume from India. During periods of football competition with teams from other schools, it was Lucasi who took the school team to the cemetery, the night before a match, with the finger of a dead man and the fresh heart of a cat which he forced the goalkeeper to eat and swallow at exactly midnight. It was even rumoured that he possessed the legendry Indian charm—the Seven Oils of Rama Krishna—that could 'magnet' any girl he desired. He had a broad forehead, a big flat face and a square aggressive jaw line. His charcoal-black complexion and catlike eyes reinforced the feline character of his mysterious face. Even at that early age in elementary school he radiated a sinister aura and moved around with an air of concealed malevolence. There was something malicious about his inscrutable, enigmatic face and the way he walked. Most boys in the school were scared of him and wanted to avoid him. But they pretended to associate with him to avoid being seen as opposing him. He ruthlessly dealt with anyone whom he perceived as an opponent. The most formidable weapon he used to subdue other boys, even those who were twice his age, was the iron grip of his right hand. The grip was like a clamp. He would grip any boy who annoyed or challenged him on the wrist and stare at the eyes of the unfortunate victim for hours, without blinking, until the ill-fated boy collapsed out of sheer exhaustion. Once he had made up his mind to humiliate an opponent, not even the strongest boy in the school or the teachers could unloosen his vice-like grip.

Saddi Tegene, in contrast, was the favourite among the teachers in the school. He was tall and handsome—a handsomeness that bothered on feminine beauty. The skin on his face was smooth and evenly stretched from his cheekbones so that when he laughed, two dimples appeared on both sides of his small mouth. He started serving mass at about the age of eight and was the lead actor in the popular end-of-year school concerts. He was always cheerful and light-hearted, all the time volunteering to help other children who were less fortunate than himself. Saddi was the only boy in the school who was not afraid of Lucasi. For some unknown reason, Lucasi avoided getting into any confrontation with him.

Although Saddi and Lucasi grew up in Bonjongo, their parents actually came from Batibo, a small town half-way between Bali and Widikum, along the Bamenda-Mamfe highway. Their parents, who lived in one of the numerous CDC work camps, were unskilled hands who had migrated to the coast and gotten recruited as labourers in the CDC plantations.

One afternoon, after school, as the children were going back home, a squabble broke out between Elio Litumbe and Veke Lucasi. Elio was in Class Seven and about thirteen years old. He was much taller, bigger, and two years older than Lucasi. The squabble started over Elio's declaration that Bijanga had smiled and fallen in love with him. The news reached Lucasi during lunch break. There was no expression

on his face when his circle of friends told him Elio's declaration. Lucasi's classmates knew 'something would happen'
when Lucasi dodged the last thirty minutes of school time
before the closing period. Shortly before closing time, the
boys split into two groups. The first group was Lucasi's classmates. They ran down the road that snaked its way through
the school orchard of papaya, mangoes, guava, and cherry
trees. The small narrow path wound its way behind the school
incinerator. It was here that they found Lucasi. He had gone
into a nearby bush and harvested some herbs that the boys
did not know. His square jaws moved up and down in a steady
regular rhythm as he chewed the herbs. His eyes were red.
He remained silent and motionless, his legs at akimbo as he
blocked the small path. The boys stopped dead in their tracks
the moment they rounded the bend behind the incinerator
and saw Lucasi blocking the small narrow path.

The second group was made up of pupils in Class Six
and Seven. They stayed behind with Elio after closing time.
They knew Elio was one of the strongest boys in the school.
They expected, in fact, wanted a confrontation between Elio
and Lucasi. They wanted someone to put an end to Lucasi's
Indian powers. Elio was powerful, bold, and fearless as he
strapped his bag over his back and began walking down in
the direction of the orchard with his supporters.

As the boys in Elio's group came round the incinerator,
they saw Lucasi barring the road. For the first time the boys
who walked with Elio hesitated. They let Elio walk some
distance ahead of them. Elio walked on without the slightest
trace of hesitation or fear when he saw Lucasi on the road.
He walked up to a metre of Lucasi and stood still. The two
boys stared at each other. The two groups of boys expected a

fight and each group was sure its 'man' would win the fight.

"Let me pass," Elio said in a challenging, defiant voice.

Lucasi did not respond. He continued chewing the leaves. His red eyes were fixed intensely on his opponent's face. After about two minutes, he spat the green mixture of spittle and leaves onto the roadside. His lips quivered momentarily before he spoke. "Everyone knows Bijanga is my girl. How come you say she loves you?"

"Liar!" Elio hissed. "She smiled at me today. She never talks to you. Why do you claim she loves you?"

"Everyone knows she's mine. No one approaches her for friendship or love." Lucasi spoke softly, unhurried.

"Let me pass, you're blocking the road," Elio said. There was a defiant sneer on his round smooth face.

"You won't go home today until you tell everyone that Bijanga is not your girl."

"Son of Lucifer!" one of the boys in Lucasi's group called out assertively. Almost immediately the rest of the boys took up the call and began chanting, "Son of Lucifer! Son of Lucifer!"

Elio raised his right hand, placed it on Lucasi's chest and pushed him. Lucasi staggered momentarily but stood his ground. Sensing some kind of victory Elio's group began chanting, "Elio, lover boy! Elio, lover boy!"

This time Elio raised both hands and was about holding Lucasi when, in a swift, rapid motion, Lucasi griped Elio's right wrist with his right hand. Elio held Lucasi's hand with his other hand and tried to pull himself out of the grip that was beginning to choke his right wrist; but his attempt to free himself only tightened Lucasi's grip on his wrist.

"Son of Lucifer!" the boys in Lucasi's group intoned. "Son

of Lucifer!"

"Let him go," one of the boys in Elio's group said. Three of the boys stepped forward and tried to unfasten Lucasi's fingers from Elio's wrist, but Lucasi's gripped remained firm. He did not as much as glance at the three boys as they struggled to untangle their friend from his grip. Lucasi's red eyes bore into Elio's eyes without blinking.

Ten minutes went by and Elio began sweating profusely. "Let me go," he said. "Leave my hand alone."

Lucasi paid no attention to his pleas. He only stared at him impassively, his eyes glazed as if he was in a trance. The other boys called his name several times, but he did not respond. He did not seem to be aware of their presence anymore. He appeared to have been transported into another dimension. Fifteen minutes went by. The boys in both groups became frightened.

It was at that moment that they heard voices approaching from the orchard. Bijanga, Saddi, two girls in Class Five, and a boy in Class Four emerged from the road behind the incinerator. The boys in Elio's group and Lucasi's friends had now surrounded Elio and Lucasi.

"What's going on here?" Saddi asked the two antagonists, turning his face from Lucasi to Elio. Elio's Adam's apple moved once as he swallowed his own spittle. He was too exhausted to utter a reply. "Do you hear me, Veke Lucasi? What kind of game are you playing?"

"It's not a game," one of the boys in Elio's camp said. "Lucasi is punishing him. He wants to subdue him. He refuses to release his wrist and we can't free Elio's hand from his grip."

Saddi came nearer and stood close to Lucasi and Elio. "Okay Veke, let him go. That's enough."

The catlike features on Lucasi's face remained immobile. His unblinking eyes bore down in his opponent's face. His gaze was relentless, ruthless. It was as if he had not heard Saddi.

"I say let him go now!" Saddi insisted. There was a trace of warning in his voice. "Don't let me step in between the two of you."

"Release the boy now!" Bijanga said. A sardonic sneer hovered around the corners of her mouth. "You heard what I said, Veke Lucasi. Let him go!" Her voice seemed to bring Lucasi out of his trance. His eyes blinked several times as he turned his head slowly to the left, in the direction of Bijanga's voice. Lucasi released Elio's wrist abruptly and pushed him violently on the chest with both hands. As Elio fell down on the ground, Lucasi walked away unceremoniously from the rest of the boys and began walking down the path away from the incinerator. His friends followed him and began chanting, "Son of Lucifer! Son of Lucifer!"

Saddi knelt down and held the boy. "Are you okay?"

Bijanga joined Saddi and held Elio's left hand. "Let's help him up." They lifted the boy to his feet.

"I'm fine," Elio said in a feeble voice. He stood up unsteadily, his knees wobbling. One by one, the rest of the children left the scene. Elio was left standing awkwardly between Saddi and Bijanga. He was ashamed of the wetness between his legs where he had urinated in his khaki shorts. He did not know whether Saddi or Bijanga had seen the wet patch between his legs. He turned first to Bijanga and said, "I want to go home now" before he turned to Saddi and said, "Thank you for helping me." Then he walked down the road in slow, unsteady strides.

After Elio left, Saddi turned to Bijanga. "You know why they were fighting, don't you?"

"I do," Bijanga said. "It was my fault. I shouldn't have laughed with Elio the way I did."

"It wasn't your fault," Saddi said. "You can laugh and play with whoever you want to. Tell me, do you love Lucasi? He claims that you're his girl."

"I don't know why he keeps on saying that I'm his girl. He has never told me that he loves me."

"All the boys know he's mad about you. Do you love him?" Saddi wanted to know.

"I don't know," Bijanga said. "I don't know whether he loves me or not? Perhaps he will tell me one day."

"And if he does, will you accept him?"

"I don't know," Bijanga said.

"And what about me?" Saddi wanted to know. "I've told you that I want to be your friend, but you've said nothing."

"That's not true. We sometimes play together, don't we? And I laugh every time we see each other."

"Playing and laughing are not enough," Saddi went on. "You should tell me something."

"What do you want me to tell you?"

Saddi kept quiet for a moment. He wondered what Bijanga should tell him. He had never thought about it? What should a girl say when a boy told her he loved her?

"Tell me anything." He felt silly and confused.

"Give me something and I will tell you whether I love you."

"Something? Like what?"

"I don't know. Anything," Bijanga said. She began walking away. "You're the one to decide."

Saddi stood alone for a long time after Bijanga had disappeared from sight. What did she mean by giving her something? How could he decide what to give her? Could Lucasi have given her something and she was hiding the truth from him? Was Lucasi telling the truth that Bijanga was his girl and no one else could lay claim to her love? If there was one thing that attracted him to Bijanga it was her eyes, her lips. No, not her lips or eyes, but her face, the way she smiled and her shinning white teeth. Now he felt more confused than ever as he walked home. What was it about Bijanga that made boys fight over her? He continued thinking about Bijanga and what she had said till he got home. He could not stop thinking about her as he did his homework.

* * *

After they graduated from Bonjongo primary school, Saddi and Lucasi were admitted into St. Joseph's College (SJC) in Buea. They considered themselves lucky to be the only boys from their primary school who gained admission into the prestigious boys' boarding school. They lost track of Bijanga soon after they went to SJC. It took just two years—when they were in Form Three—for Lucasi to establish himself as a conjurer in the college. He received a catalogue from an Ashram in Madras during the first term in Form Three. The catalogue contained pictures and addresses of talismans and brain pills that could accelerate the learning capacities of students and help them pass their exams. It was during the second term that Lucasi received The *Six and Seven Books of Moses* and *The Seven Keys to Power* from India. It was after Lucasi received the two books that he began 'performing magic' in the college. The subjects of his conjuring experiments were, most often, Form One students from whose ears, armpits, and buttocks he conjured eggs, biscuits, and sweets, much to the delight of the students who ate the goodies that Lucasi pulled out from their bodies. By the middle of the third term Lucasi had become quite popular with the school prefects and Form Five students who wanted to master the secrets of charming girls and ordering brain pills from India to help them pass their exams.

Saddi stayed casual friends with Lucasi, keeping a distance from Lucasi's magical reputation. Their five-year stay in SJC was almost uneventful except for the Henry Sako incident when Lucasi was nearly dismissed in Form Four. On that particular day Rev. Father Flynn, the Irish missionary priest who was principal of the college, summoned Lucasi to appear before the disciplinary council to answer charges of 'unethical misconduct antithetical to SJC's Catholic and Christian character.'

One week before the G.C.E. exams began in June, Henry Sako, a Form Five student from Victoria who had acquired brain pills from Lucasi, began behaving strangely. First, he began by imitating the principal's funny Irish accent, telling students in his dormitory that he was now the principal of SJC. The students laughed, taking it as one of his usual jokes. The following day, he stripped himself naked in the dormitory and began repeating the strange mantra, "Majid-Kashmikar-Hal, Majid-Kashmikar-Hal" over and over. He did not go to the chapel for morning devotion; neither did he go to the refectory for breakfast and lunch. And he did not attend Prep classes in the evening either. When the students came back to the dormitory at 9 PM, they found him standing on his head in front of his bed, still reciting the strange mantra, "Majid-Kashmikar-Hal." That was when the Senior Prefect called the school nurse, Mrs Kandem, who in turn went to get the discipline master, Mr Sabum, to see Sako's strange behaviour. They carried him to the infirmary where he was given a tranquiliser and kept under observation for the night.

Mrs Kandem rushed out of the infirmary at about 2 AM, locked the main door with the key, and ran to the discipline's master's house. She pounded his front door with her fist. Mr Sabum came out dressed in his pyjamas. His wife too was up. She kept a close distance behind her husband. Mr Sabum opened the door and saw the nurse's frightened face illuminated by the light of the single fluorescent security bulb in his corridor.

"What's the matter, Mrs Kandem?" Mr Sabum asked.

"Sako's situation has worsened, Sir. Something terrible is happening to him. The principal has to be informed at once."

"You know the college regulations, Mrs Kandem. We first of all have to inform the House Master, who in turn must inform the vice-principal before Father Flynn is—"

"There is no time for that now, sir. It's no longer a school case. The boy's parents have to be contacted right away so they can take him to a competent medical institution."

The discipline master noticed that Mrs Kandem's hands were shaking and her usually placid face was pale with fear. The fright on the nurse's face made him forget that he was dressed in pyjamas. He asked his wife to close the door behind him as he walked back to the infirmary with Mrs Kandem.

Mrs Kandem opened the door of the infirmary slowly and allowed Mr Sabum to go in first. When Mr Sabum saw the boy he said, "Oh my God! What has happened to him?"

He stepped back from the room and asked the nurse to lock the door. "We have to get the principal right away. There's no time to lose."

It took them only five minutes to reach Father Flynn's house. Mr Sabum banged on Father Flynn's front door and announced this name.

"What the hell is going on?" Father Flynn asked in his Irish accent. They heard him cursing and muttering something about three in the morning. When he came out, his face was red and he was dressed in a black house coat.

"I'm sorry, Father," Mr Sabum apologized. "We have an emergency in the infirmary. One of the Form Five boys is in bad shape. We don't know what's happened to him."

"I administered him a tranquiliser at about nine in the night and kept him in the infirmary for observation," Mrs Kandem tried to explain. "He's not the same boy I admitted in the infirmary last night."

"Rubbish! Can't understand you two," Father Flynn said. Noticing that the discipline master had lost his composure and the nurse looked frightened, he said, "Auw right. Let me put on my slippers." He went back to the house, put on his slippers, and the three of them walked back to the infirmary.

Mrs Kandem handed the key to Father Flynn. "I'm afraid to go in there, Father."

"What nonsense! Have you lost your head?"

Father Flynn seized the key from her, opened the door and stepped into the infirmary. Mr Sabum and the nurse followed cautiously behind.

"Jesus Christ!" Father Flynn exclaimed when he saw the boy. He made the sign of the cross as he spoke. "I should have been told earlier than now."

Sako had left the bed on which he lay. He was now coiled up on the floor with his head contorted in between his legs. His arms were intertwined around his neck and in-between his feet, so much that he looked like a human ball on the floor. Father Flynn was taken aback by the boy's face. Isolated patches of white hair had sprouted on his face, cheeks, chin, and upper neck. He was groaning and still muttering, "Majid-Kashmikar-Hal, "Majid-Kashmikar-Hal."

Father Flynn ran to his house and came back with his car in just under seven minutes. Mr Sabum called the Senior Prefect and two other big boys who helped bundle Sako into the principal's car and restrained him with a seat belt. Mrs Kandem and Mr Sabum entered the car. Father Flynn drove the car out of the campus and headed towards the Mount Mary hospital in Soppo.

Two weeks later the cause of Sako's mysterious transformation was traced to pills from Lucasi that allegedly originated from India. Lucasi's locker and box were thoroughly searched by the Vice Principal. No pills or anything suspicious were found in the locker. But the students in his dormitory knew the truth. Lucasi had moved his magic books and bottle of brain pills to St. Christopher's dormitory thirty minutes before the search.

Lucasi was summoned to appear before the disciplinary council the next day at 2 PM. Rumour was rife that he would be dismissed. Lucasi did not sleep in the dormitory that night. He collected *The Six and Seven Books of Moses* and *The Seven Keys to Power* from St. Christopher's dormitory and went to the refectory where he spent the whole night conjuring and binding the principal and members of the disciplinary council. He came back to his dormitory around five thirty in the morning.

His appearance before the council the next day was brief. The discipline master and the V.P. conducted the interrogation.

"Are you in possession of any kind of pills from India?" the V.P. asked him.

"No, sir," Lucasi replied.

"Do you know what has happened to Henry Sako?"

"Yes, sir. I understand he's been taken to the hospital."

"Did you give him any kind of medication?"

"Yes, sir. I did."

"You did?" The V.P. and two members of the Disciplinary Council leaned forward. "What kind of medication?"

Lucasi reached inside his pocket and brought out a small bottle. He stood up, walked deliberately towards Mrs Kandem and handed her the bottle. "*Paracetamol*, sir," he said without any expression on his countenance. He glanced at the faces of the seven members of the disciplinary council and added, "Sako complained of a headache when he came back to the dormitory after Prep. I gave him twelve tablets of *Parac-etamol*. I now realize I shouldn't have. I should have asked him to see the nurse instead. Perhaps he took an overdose, I don't know." He walked back to the single chair in front of the disciplinary council and sat down. Then he added, "I'm quite sorry."

"Are you in possession of any magic books?" the V.P. continued with the interrogation.

"No, sir. Not to my knowledge. Except ... Well, I possess—"

Father Flynn leaned forward. Despite himself he said, "Yes, what kind of books?"

"The College Bible, Father. Good News for Modern Man." Some members of the council laughed. There was a stony look on the V.P.'s face.

"Are you a magician, Veke Lucasi?" the V.P. continued.

"No, sir. I'm not."

"But you perform strange tricks on junior students, don't you?"

"Yes, sir. I do."

"If that's not magic, what's it then?" Mr Sabum wanted to know.

"Tricks, sir. Simple tricks to amuse the students."

There was a twinkle of amusement on Father Flynn's eyes. "Can you show us some of your so-called conjuring tricks?"

"Yes, Father, yes. I'll be delighted to." Lucasi stood up and took a few steps closer to the members of the council. He made a quick bow before he raised his right hand and showed it to the disciplinary council. It was empty. He said 'Abracadabra' three times, waved his hand in the air and appeared to pull something out of the empty space in front of him. When he opened his hand, there was an egg in it.

"Clever! Very clever indeed!" Father Flynn said laughing. "Clever trick all right."

"Can I see the egg?" Mr Sabum demanded.

"Yes, sir." Lucasi walked up to the discipline master and gave him the egg.

While the astonished members of the disciplinary council were examining the egg, Lucasi reached inside his pocket and brought out a spotless white handkerchief. He held the handkerchief with both hands and flapped it in the air, showing it to the council members. He folded it into a bunch and placed it on his left hand as he murmured some arcane phrases and passed his right hand seven times in the air over the hand-kerchief. Then, he pulled away the white handkerchief from his left hand. To the utmost astonishment of everyone in the room, a small sunbird was left standing on his left hand. It chirped twice, flapped its wings uncertainly, before it flew out through a window.

Father Flynn's face turned red. "Goodness me!" he exclaimed. "How the hell did you do that?"

"It's the devil's work!" Mrs Kandem began shouting. "The boy's the devil himself!"

"Auw right," Father Flynn said, turning to Mrs Kandem, "enough of that devil stuff." He turned his head and nodded in Lucasi's direction. "You can go now."

Lucasi bowed respectfully and said, "Thank you, Father" before he walked out of the room. When he got outside he took out the white handkerchief from his pocket and wiped the beads of perspiration that had accumulated on his face and neck. He knew it was a close call. As he walked back to his dormitory he made up his mind not to perform any magic tricks in the campus or use his magical books again in the college.

After he graduated from SJC, Lucasi was refused admission into the high school section but was admitted into CCAST Bambili. Because of his exemplary conduct and character in SJC and his brilliant O level performance, Saddi was allowed to continue in the two-year, second cycle of SJC for his A levels. Saddi lost touch with Lucasi after their admission into high school. But he got occasional letters from his friends in CCAST that Lucasi's magical powers had increased tenfold. It was rumoured that Lucasi had ordered a PND (Purse Never Dry) from India which guaranteed him an endless supply of money all year round. He also carried out a miraculous performance in Bambili which was witnessed by more than fifty students. During a heavy downpour he stepped out into the rain from the school refectory and walked unhurriedly to the administrative block without getting wet. When he got to the Admin Block (as the students called it) there wasn't a drop of water on his head, clothes, or shoes. An invisible umbrella had protected him from the rain as he walked between both buildings. One student claimed he had seen an arm in the air next to Lucasi as he walked in the rain.

It was in Upper Six that Saddi was told Lucasi's magical skills were now comparable only to those of D.D. Mbah in Kumba who could cut a box in two containing a woman and later put the two halves of the woman together in front of a live audience. Just before their GCE A level exams in June, Saddi received a letter from a close friend in Bambili that informed him Lucasi had received the midnight initiation into the Marantha Spider Ashram in India. The Marantha spider initiation was the pinnacle in mystical powers that any black magician could attain. Saddi was certain that Lucasi had reached the apex of his search for spiritual powers. He had now fully acquired the supernatural powers he had been searching for all these years, powers which, as he claimed, would elevate him to the position of a revered super mortal on earth.

Shortly after he graduated from high school, Saddi got a scholarship to read Accountancy at the University of Wisconsin, Eau Claire, in the U.S. Before he left for the U.S., Saddi heard Lucasi had been admitted into a Ghanaian university. When he got to the States, he lost track of Lucasi.

It was by chance in Yaoundé, the capital city, ten years

after he returned from the U.S, that Saddi bumped into Bijanga. At first he was not quite sure whether it was Bijanga. He was eye-shopping in Casino that afternoon when he saw a familiar face he had known many years ago. The woman was standing in the cosmetic section of the supermarket, holding a small shopping basket in her left hand. One of the sales girls walked up to her and said something. The woman smiled. It was that stunning smile and the dazzling whiteness of her teeth that made Saddi take a close look at the face. It must be Bijanga, he thought. He disliked embarrassing himself in front of strangers, so he waited until the woman left the checkout counter and was walking across the car park. That was when he pretended to cough and said, "Excuse me, can I help you with your bag?" The woman stopped briefly and turned around. He was damned if it wasn't Bridget Bijanga.

"Bridget?" he asked with hesitation. "Bridget Bijanga?"

"Yes?" the woman responded. "How can I …. Wait a minute. You look familiar. That must be …" She hesitated for a moment, as she tried to match the face to a name in her memory bank. "Bonjongo!" she said suddenly. "Bonjongo primary school. Tegene!" she exclaimed. "Saddi Tegene! Oh, my God! It's more than twenty years now. I wouldn't have recognized you."

Unsure of what next to say Saddi said, "Can I help you with your shopping bag?"

"Of course," she said. Then she quickly added, "Always the gentleman that you were, aren't you? Over this way. My car is parked at the far end of the parking lot."

They walked across the parking lot and came to a red Toyota Celica. Her driver was sitting patiently behind the steering wheel. She opened the front right door, took the bag of groceries from Saddi and placed it on the seat before she closed the door.

"Where have you been all these years? Do you live in Yaoundé now?"

"No," Saddi said. "I'm just visiting. From Limbe. Actually, I was in the U.S. I came back six months ago. I'm job-hunting. That's what brought me to Yaoundé."

"Bush faller, huh. Well, get into the back seat. Which direction are you headed to. I live in Madagascar, not too far from Cité Verte. I can drop you somewhere."

She opened the right back door and got into the car. Saddi went round, opened the car door behind the driver and closed the door. The driver manoeuvred the car through the narrow parking lanes and came out on the 20th May Boulevard. He turned right and drove the car in the direction of the Hilton hotel. Saddi stole a glance at her left hand to see if she wore a ring. The fingers of her left hand had no rings. Apart from the red lipstick on her lips her face was without make up. Her dark shinny hair had grown down to her back. She pinned it into a pony-tail just below her neck and allowed the rest of it to fall on her shoulders.

"I live in Biyem-Assi with my cousin," Saddi said. "I was eye-shopping when I saw you. I wasn't quite sure it was you. I'm glad I took the risk to ask."

"You always took risks, come to think of it."

"You haven't lost your charm and beauty," Saddi continued reflectively. "You still have that dazzling smile that made the knees of the boys go weak every time you laughed. You must be married now."

"Married? What makes you think I'm married? Real men are hard to come by these days. I'm still single," she added with a smile. "Just about clocking thirty-two and still waiting for Mr Right. What about you? I bet you came back home with a beautiful African American chick."

"I almost did," Saddi admitted, "but changed plans at the last moment. I prefer our women here. A foreign woman will never adapt to our traditions and way of life."

The car was getting near the Hilton. "I see. Can I drop you at Biyem-Assi?" she offered.

"Well, that's very kind of you. We can have a drink somewhere, can't we?" he suggested. He did not know what made him say it.

She glanced at him momentarily and smiled. "Why not? Stephen, take us to the Rosita restaurant." The driver nursed the car towards the Warda junction. "It's a clean, quiet place. The service there is good."

When they got to Rosita and the waiter came to their table, Bijanga said, "I'll take a Malta. What will you have for a drink? Come on, don't be embarrassed."

"I'll have a small Guinness."

The bill's on me," she told the waiter. "It will take you a while to get a job. And I guess the few dollars you brought back are finished. I didn't tell you I work with Citi Bank. The salary is good," she added. "I work in the credit department."

When the waiter brought the drinks she said, "I'm hungry. What's on your menu for this afternoon?" The waiter picked up the menu from a nearby table and gave it to her. She looked at it momentarily and raised her head. "I'll have smoked Bar fish with mixed vegetables and fried plantains. Saddi, please have something. I hate to eat alone."

"I'll have the same dish," Saddi said.

"Are you sure? You can choose something else."

"I'm quite sure."

"Waiter, two dishes please."

They tried to catch up with the years as they ate. Saddi told her about his ten-year stay in the U.S., that he first of all did a BA in Accountancy and later an MBA. She said she read Economics at the local university in Yaoundé. She talked about her connections in the Ministry of Finance and wondered what kind of position Saddi had in mind.

"A job that will require my accountancy and management skills," Saddi said.

"Wait a minute. How could I forget? You remember Lucasi, don't you?"

"Veke Lucasi? Of course, I do. Is he here in Yaoundé?"

"Yes. You were classmates in SJC, weren't you? Well, he's a big shot in the Ministry of Finance. Director of salaries, actually. There will soon be vacancies in his ministry."

"Don't say."

"Today is Saturday. Come by to Citi Bank opposite the British Council on Wednesday next week at twelve. I have a one-hour lunch break. We'll drive up to the Ministry and see Lucasi. Boy-oh-boy, I'll love to see the look on his face when he sees you."

Saddi emptied the rest of the Guinness into his glass and drank half of the glass before he said, "I'm looking forward to seeing him again." He didn't know why he felt uneasy at the thought of meeting Lucasi. Then he added, "It will certainly be a memorable reunion."

"Lucasi will be surprised to see you again after all these years." She beckoned the waiter to bring the bill.

The following week Saddi got to Citi Bank on Wednesday fifteen minutes before midday. Bijanga came out of the bank exactly at twelve. Her driver pulled the car out of the bank's parking lot, turned right and drove towards the central post office. When the lights at the post office roundabout changed to green, the car took another right turn behind *Camtel* and headed up towards the ministry of finance. Stephen parked the car in front of the Ministry of Agriculture. Bijanga flashed her Citi Bank professional card to the security guards and entered the ministry with Saddi. When they got into Lucasi's secretariat on the fourth floor, the secretary said he was busy.

"How busy is he?" Bijanga wanted to know.

"He's in a meeting right now. He can't receive anyone."

Bijanga reached inside her handbag and brought out a pen. "Let me have a request for audience form."

"Audience for when and for what?" the secretary wanted to know.

"For Friday," Bijanga said.

The secretary picked up a form from a tray and gave it to Bijanga. Bijanga wrote a brief note on the paper, brought out a complimentary card from her handbag, picked up a paper clip from the secretary's table and attached her complimentary card to the 'request for audience' form. "Here," she said, "give this to him right away."

The secretary took the form and card, hesitated momentarily and then stood up. She came out from behind her desk, opened the director's door and closed it behind her.

Saddi glanced at Bijanga from where he sat. He looked ill at ease.

"What's the problem?" Bijanga asked.

"I was just wondering. We should have made an appointment."

"I did, actually."

"Why didn't you just tell her we had an appointment with her boss?"

Bijanga smiled. "To let you see how the system works. I've come here several times. I think she recognises me, but she's pretending she doesn't know me. She probably wants me to grease her palms with some money before she allows me to see the director. She's in for a surprise."

The secretary came out as they spoke. She looked apologetic. "I'm sorry, *Madame*," she said. "The Director will receive both of you right away. Next time please tell me who you are so that I don't keep you waiting." She ushered them into the director's cabinet and closed the door behind them.

Veke Lucasi stood up as they walked into his spacious office. He was dressed in a flawless black suit that blended with his dark complexion. He looked aloof and distant with a cold calculated stare on his face as he appraised Saddi momentarily. His mannerism was deliberate, purposeful. He walked up to Bijanga and kissed her lightly on both cheeks. Then he shook hands briefly with Saddi. He asked both of them to sit down and asked whether they would have tea or coffee. Bijanga said coffee. Saddi said tea. Lucasi called the secretary and asked her to bring two cups of coffee and a cup of tea. As they sipped the hot beverages, Lucasi went straight to the point of the meeting. He made no mention of their primary school days or SJC.

"Bridget tells me you need a job," Lucasi said after a brief moment of uncomfortable silence. "I understand you read accountancy and obtained an MBA in the States."

"I did, yes," Saddi said.

"There're five vacancies coming up in the ministry next month. One of them fits your educational profile. Send in your application to the minister of finance as soon as possible, in the next two or three days or so. Bridget will show you the Cameroonian way of writing applications. It has to be handwritten. Here's the list of documents you need, including fiscal stamps for each document. Anything else?"

"No," Bijanga said. "That's fine. I'll show him what to do."

Saddi took the paper containing the list of application documents from Lucasi and looked uncertainly at Bijanga.

"I'm sorry," Lucasi said impassively. "I should have talked about the good all days. All that kind of stuff. Well, I don't function like that any longer. And besides, we're quite busy in this section of the ministry. Let me know if you need additional assistance with the application."

He stood up. Bijanga and Saddi too stood up. He saw them to the door leading to his secretariat and closed the door gently behind them. The secretary apologised again as she saw them out of the secretariat.

As soon as they came out into the corridor Saddi asked, "What's wrong with him? Why did he act so strangely as if he only knew us last week? You think I'll get the job? I'm not quite sure he'll allow me to be recruited in the ministry."

Bijanga laughed. "Don't worry, you'll be recruited. He's been like this for some years now. He doesn't talk about the past. Some people are like that, you know. You'll get used to him."

Saddi was recruited into the ministry of finance three months later. Six months after his recruitment into the ministry, he was appointed deputy director of salaries, a post that had been vacant for three years following the death of the previous deputy director. It did not take long for Saddi to develop a relationship with Bijanga. Initially it was casual.

Once in a while they went out for lunch. Occasionally Saddi invited Bijanga to watch a movie at Abbia on Saturdays.

One weekend Bijanga invited him for lunch at her apartment in Madagascar. He had never been to Madagascar before, but he followed her directions and drove to the gas station opposite the junction descending to Cité Verte. He called her cell phone and told her where he was. In less than ten minutes she was at the fuel station. He didn't see her until she tapped his car's side screen. When he turned his head, he was dazzled by her smile and flashing white teeth. She wore a multi-coloured *kabba* outfit that was dominated by pink and blue. The *kabba* was loose on her body but designed to fit snugly over her chest, outlining the contours of her full-sized breasts. She got into the car and directed him to drive about a hundred metres along a small narrow access road from the filling station. When they got to her apartment, he was surprised at how modest she lived. There was not much in the apartment apart from two large paintings with expensive frames, a Mahogany dining table and cane chairs, a Sony CD musical set, a 17-inch flat TV and wooden side stools.

"This is a beautiful place," Saddi remarked as he sat down. "A touch of class. Quite modest indeed."

"Thank you," Bijanga said. "I like it this way. Can I get you something to drink before I serve lunch?"

"A small Guinness will do, thanks."

"I only have a large bottle left in the fridge."

"A large bottle will be fine."

She went into the kitchen and closed the door behind her. When she emerged from the kitchen, she found him standing up, examining the paintings. She placed the tray on the dining table. He turned around momentarily and noticed that there was a large jar of freshly squeezed grapefruit juice, two glasses, and a bottle of Guinness on the tray.

"Here's your Guinness. Would you have it on a side stool?"

"I didn't know you had homemade juice. I prefer it to the Guinness, if you don't mind."

"Oh, not at all. So long as it's not a forced conversion," she said laughing. "I know you men like beer."

She took the Guinness back to the kitchen, and while he sipped the juice, she started serving lunch. Ten minutes later, with soft CD music in the background, she invited him to the dining table and they began eating. In between mouthfuls, he kept on muttering "You're a wonderful cook. I haven't eaten anything like this for a long while." She responded to his compliments with an occasional throaty chuckle and a generous smile. When they finished eating, she cleared the table and carried the dishes to the kitchen. He went back to his original sitting position in the living room and sat down heavily. When Bijanga came back from the kitchen, she changed the CDs in the musical set before she sat down next to Saddi.

"The food was so good that I overindulged myself. I'm afraid I've eaten more than my stomach can handle."

"Well, I am glad you like my cooking. Will you have another glass of juice? It won't do you any harm."

"If you insist."

She stood up, went to fetch the juice and came back. She poured a full glass and pushed the side table a little bit closer to him. He did not know why the thought of her being single kept on occupying his mind. He was prepared to make a definite proposition to her, a clear unambiguous declaration that will make her understand the intense feeling he was developing for her, an emotional desire that was increasing in passionate intensity. He searched desperately for an excuse that will make him declare his affection for her. Quite suddenly, out of nowhere, he thought of Veke Lucasi. He found it inconceivable that Lucasi would be in the same city all these years without making a proposal to her.

He turned his head slightly and looked at her. "Does Lucasi know where you live?" he asked suddenly without any expression on his face. "Has he been here before?"

"Lucasi?" Bijanga looked surprised. "Why? What's that got to do with your coming over here for lunch this afternoon?"

Sooner or later she knew Saddi would enquire about her relationship with Lucasi. But she had not anticipated it would come up so abruptly. She was prepared to handle it. But she did not know whether she should be tactful or reckless in her response. For now, she decided to be frank and up front. The best way to confront any difficulty was to be sincere and straightforward. She had nothing to hide. Was it their old rivalry in Bonjongo that was surfacing again in Yaoundé after all these years? Her heart had missed a beat the day she saw him at the parking lot in Casino. Why for Christ's sake had she met Saddi again? What had brought him to Yaoundé? She knew she had made a terrible blunder the moment she decided to take him to meet Lucasi at the ministry. There was nothing she could do now. She only had to see what would happen, how the events would unfold.

"You seem to be intimately familiar with Lucasi," Saddi said, "but I've never seen both of you together all these months I've been in Yaoundé."

She pretended to be upset. "Do you feel threatened by my familiarity with him?" she demanded. "To answer your question, I say yes. We're friends. Very good friends. We've known ourselves now for more than five years. I've invited him over to my apartment several times in fact."

"You have?"

"Yes. When I lived in *Nlongkak*, when I moved to Cité Verte, and when I moved here to Madagascar. I can't remember how many times I've asked him to come over here for lunch or dinner on weekends. But he made up one excuse or the other. It's either his work at the ministry, travelling with the minister or something else. For Christ's sake, Saddi, I knew this guy long ago in primary school. It's been exciting knowing him as a big shot, a director in the ministry of finance. And out of nowhere you appear suddenly in Yaoundé. And here you are, asking me about Lucasi. What do you expect me to say?"

"You don't have to be upset—"

"Put yourself in my shoes. Wouldn't you be upset?"

"I didn't mean to," Saddi began to apologise. "I don't know how to put this to you."

"Say whatever it is you want to say. I'm all ears."

He hesitated for a moment. He knew Bridget was already upset. He didn't want to continue offending her. He took a deep breath and said, "There's something about you I can't resist. The moment I saw you at Casino I knew it. Lucasi too has the same feelings for you, I suppose."

"Talk about yourself and leave Lucasi out of whatever you want to say. Saddi, you've not changed after all these years. Still the same old jealous romantic you were in primary school. Well, I'll be frank with you about Lucasi."

She went to the bedroom and came back shortly half-dragging, half-pulling a battered suitcase after her. She put the suitcase near the dining table and pointed at it.

"Unzip the case and open it."

"What's in it?"

"Just do it!"

Saddi stood up and unzipped the suitcase. It was full of assorted boxes all carefully wrapped up in expensive gift paper and coloured ribbons. Saddi looked at her.

"Gifts? How many of them are in the suitcase?"

"I don't know how many. I've lost count. Lucasi has virtually swamped me with these presents for the last three years. He seizes every occasion to send me a present. My birthday, Christmas, Youth day, 20th May, Easter, Women's day, Mother's day, even though I'm not a mother. You name it. He's inundated me with gifts. In the first year I opened every one of them. Then I started giving them out to friends and relatives. All kinds of expensive perfumes. Wines I've never drunk or will ever drink. Gold and rhinestone jewellery. Gorgeous dresses and suits. Make-up sets from Europe and the U.S. At the onset, I felt honoured to be accorded this unusual attention, so one day I asked him to come over to my place for dinner. I cooked some of the best dishes I've ever cooked and doused myself with one of his expensive perfumes. I was surprised when he declined my invitation. But his gifts continued. And I began feeling suffocated. Two years ago, I stopped opening the presents. But he kept on sending them. There are three more suitcases in the room filled with his presents. I don't know what to do or say."

"Have you tried to discuss it with him?"

"I tried to. Last year. Six months before you showed up in Yaoundé, I went to his office and decided to tell him to stop sending me these ridiculously expensive presents. He simply dismissed the discussion and went on to something else. After a while he told me he was going upstairs for a meeting with the minister. I don't think he intends to discuss it."

"Quite obviously Lucasi is madly in love with you, but for some strange reason, he hasn't got the guts to tell you so. And where does that leave me? Look, Bridget, if there's one woman I am going to marry, that woman is you."

He moved closer, held her chin with his right hand, lifted her head slowly and kissed her. Bijanga looked at his gentle eyes for a while and wrapped her long arms around him, clasping him in a friendly hug. She stared at the painting opposite her as she savoured the ecstatic spasms that rippled down her body. It was a long time; a very long time that she had held a man so close to her. When she released him there was a mixture of expectation and uncertainty on her face.

She could feel his very thoughts. "I know," she said. "You don't have to say it. Sooner or later I'll have to make up my mind."

It was close to 4 PM when Saddi left her apartment. For the first time in his life he felt contented. It was a strange, light-hearted feeling, difficult to explain. He had never felt like this before. My God, what a woman! Somewhere in the distant future he saw his children. Three girls and a boy. The girls all looking like Bridget, with the genetic disposition of her dazzling white teeth and that alluring, enigmatic smile. The boy looked a little more like him, with his mother's forehead and chin. He began whistling as he drove along the Madagascar Avenue towards central town to *Mahima* supermarket where he wanted to shop for groceries.

Bijanga was surprised the following week, on Wednesday, when Lucasi called her on her cell phone and insisted on a dinner appointment for Friday evening. She accepted the invitation. They would meet at the Hilton hotel at six forty-five in the evening. He was there on time, probably fifteen or twenty minutes before she arrived. He was waiting for her in front of the hotel lobby when she emerged from the car. Her driver eased the car into a parking space away from the lobby when she left the car. Lucasi, as usual, was well-groomed and looked elegant in his dark-grey suit, red tie and polished black shoes. They first had a cocktail, then shrimp salad with oyster sauce. The next course was oven-baked sole and fried rice mixed with vegetables. He drank a sweetened white wine during the meal, while she insisted on having fresh guava juice. She knew this unusual invitation for dinner, after all these years, will mark a significant turn in their relationship. Something was certainly up his sleeve. She tried not to think about it or guess what it would be, but she knew it would be big. She wasn't too surprised when he took out a small velvet box from one of his jacket pockets. He placed the box on the table, snapped it open, and turned it to face her. It was an engagement ring. The moment she looked at it, she knew it was an expensive diamond ring.

Lucasi looked at her and said, "You know what it means, don't you?"

"I do, yes. You don't expect me to try it here, do you? You've not given me a chance to make up my mind or say something."

"You don't have to. You've had all these years to make up your mind."

The diamond on the ring reflected the dim lights in the restaurant. She pulled the small case toward her and closed it shut. "I'll take it home," she said. "You have to give me time,

Lucasi. This is a major decision I have to take. I haven't had much time to think about marriage, not less marrying you."

"You have all the time in the world," Lucasi said. "But you won't take for ever, I am sure."

He looked at his watch. Bijanga recognised the bureaucratic gesture for what it was. Dinner and his time for her this evening were over. She stood up. Lucasi walked her to her car. As her driver started the engine and began driving away she looked up and saw his dark face. For a moment she thought she noticed tiny beads of perspiration on his dark broad forehead. She may have been mistaken. Lucasi's face was impassive and unemotional as the car drove away from the Hilton. He waved his right hand mechanically at the indistinct contour of her silhouette that was receding with the departing car.

Bijanga felt obliged to let Saddi know this unusual development with Lucasi. She asked Saddi to come to her apartment at Madagascar on Saturday. Saddi perceived a trace of apprehension in her voice as he talked to her on his cell phone. She was uneasy and agitated when he got to her apartment at 4 PM.

"Good God!" Saddi exclaimed the moment he stepped into the living room and saw the look on her face. She was pale and worried. "What's going on? You look terrible."

She did not even ask him to sit down before she went to the bedroom. She came back shortly with the small velvet case containing the diamond ring. She opened it and showed it to him.

"An engagement ring?" Saddi knew where it came from even before he said "Who gave it to you?"

"Lucasi invited me for dinner at the Hilton last weekend.

He took me unawares when he gave me the ring. He wants me to marry him."

"What did you say?"

"I told him he should give me time to think about it."

"Time to think about it? You don't feel committed to me then?"

"Of course I do, Saddi. Lucasi gave me no chance to think. There's a strange force around him whenever I'm with him. I don't know what it is, but I feel powerless against him. I don't know where I got the strength to resist putting on the ring in the restaurant."

Saddi began pacing the room as he tried to think. It was not by accident that Lucasi had given Bridget the engagement ring, barely a week after he had proposed to her. But how did he know? He was now convinced Lucasi was using his mystical powers and spreading his supernatural tentacles in the night, finding out what his friends and foes were doing and thinking. He realised now why most of Lucasi's subordinates were scared of him. Workers in the ministry avoided him when he walked along the corridors. He had heard rumours in the ministry that even the minister was afraid of him. Lucasi had become a monster, a dangerous ulcer that was slowly eating away its victim's entrails. Attempting to treat the ulcer would kill the patient. Only a radical operation would save the situation. There were no alternatives. He must confront Lucasi, like he had done several years ago in Bonjongo when Lucasi had gripped Elio's hand and had almost overpowered the poor boy to death.

Lucasi lived in Bastos, the affluent neighbourhood where diplomats, prosperous businessmen, top civil servants, and professional fraudsters (oftentimes called feymen) lived.

Saddi arrived there fifteen minutes after nine in the morning the following day. The security guard checked his ID before he opened the gate. Saddi drove his car into the spacious courtyard adorned with flowers and plants. A male servant came outside and ushered him into the living room through the front terrace.

"The director will be with you in a moment, sir. Please have a sit. Can I offer you something to drink?"

"It's okay Jean-Pierre. I'll serve him myself." It was Lucasi. He emerged from the study wearing a blue track suit and white tennis shoes. He appeared to have been expecting Saddi. "Leave us alone for a while."

"Okay sir. Thank you," Jean-Pierre said. He turned to Saddi and bowed his head. "Have a good day, *Monsieur*."

Saddi was still standing. The servant left as Lucasi walked across the living room. He did not shake hands with Saddi. A faint sardonic smile hovered momentarily around the corners of Lucasi's mouth as he said, "Please sit down." Saddi sat down on one of the plush leather chairs. Lucasi sat down on another chair opposite him. "As you can see, I was getting ready to go for tennis. I thought you would be in church. What brings you here so early this Sunday morning?"

"You should know why I'm here," Saddi retorted. His brow was constricted in a frown. He felt like throwing a punch on Lucasi's face, but he struggled to control himself.

"Why should I? You tell me."

"You gave Bridget an engagement ring last week, didn't you?"

Lucasi did not answer. His eyes were riveted on Saddi's face for close to half a minute. His countenance remained calm and expressionless. If he was surprised it did not show on his face.

"Did you, or did you not?"

"And if I did, what has that got to do with you? Since when did you become Bridget's errand boy?" Then almost immediately he added, "Asking me about the engagement ring serves no useful purpose. Sooner or later she has to decide who she will marry."

"She has already decided," Saddi said vehemently.

"She has, has she?" Lucasi demanded. A faint contemptuous grin appeared again on one corner of his mouth. "Did she say she'll marry you? Come on, tell me."

Saddi remained silent. Bijanga had not made any concrete statement when he mentioned marriage. He wondered why she sounded ambivalent, why she had taken the engagement ring in the first place if she had no feelings for Lucasi.

Lucasi appeared to be reading his thoughts. "Ah, I see doubt and hesitation enveloping your mind like a thick fog. I feel sorry for you, my friend. You don't seem to have mastered the psychology of women all these years. Our women are not like those American women you got so used to before coming back home. By the way let me get you a drink. I know it's rather early to start drinking beer. I have fruit juices and soft drinks in the fridge."

"I don't want your drink," Saddi said.

Lucasi grinned briefly. "You're scared I'll poison you, aren't you? No, my friend, I'm not that kind of person. I'll get a glass of orange juice for myself." He stood up. "Just two or three minutes and I'll be back." He went towards the kitchen, opened the kitchen door and closed it behind him.

Apart from their heated exchange, there was something else that seemed to upset Saddi. He wondered what it was.

He stood up from the chair and began walking around in the room. All of a sudden his nostrils picked up a stench and twitched involuntarily. That was when he discovered what it was that upset him. It was the smell in the house. The living room smelt of something evil. A strong disgusting odour had enveloped him the moment he stepped into the living room. He continued looking round the room. He was shocked when he noticed an enormous spider web hidden in a corner behind a small cupboard at the far end of the room. His first thought was that it was an artificial web, a decoration intended to adorn the living room, much like the artificial flowers Chinese hawkers sold in shops and street corners. But he couldn't remember seeing artificial spider webs in Chinese shops anywhere in town. He edged nearer and took a close look at the web. Yes, the odour was emanating from this end of the room. It was at that moment that he saw the spider. It was a huge black spider, much bigger than a tarantula. It was hidden at one corner of the web. It was so still that he thought it was part of the decoration. He raised his right hand slowly and stretched his finger forward. He wanted to touch the web and see whether the spider will move. To his greatest astonishment, as if to answer his thoughts, the spider began crawling slowly towards the centre of the web.

He was so captivated and hypnotized by what he saw that he didn't hear Lucasi open the kitchen door and enter the living room. His hand was still raised in the air when he heard Lucasi scream. The tray dropped from Lucasi's hands and the glass shattered on the floor. Lucasi sprang towards him and pushed him violently away from the web. "You damned bloody intruding bastard! What the hell do you think you're doing?"

Saddi fell down on the carpet. He was greatly shaken by what he had seen. He felt slightly dizzy. His mind seemed to be swimming in some dark haze. Lucasi bent down and tried to help him up.

"Don't touch me!" Saddi hissed. He stood up by himself and sat on a chair. He felt his head throbbing. He held his head with his right hand and closed his eyes briefly. When he opened his eyes, he saw Lucasi sitting on a chair. He appeared to have regained his composure. He apologised for his strange behaviour.

"Is that … is that a real spider and spider web?" Saddi asked.

"Yes. It's a pet spider I got from India. I thought you wanted to touch it. You shouldn't have gone there."

Saddi stood up. "I have to go now." He did not wait for Lucasi to see him out. He walked quickly through the front terrace and got to his car. The security guard opened the gate and he drove out of the compound.

It was two weeks after their confrontation that the idea of killing Lucasi first occurred to Saddi. The more he thought about it, the more he convinced himself that he had to do away with him. And he had to do it quickly and inconspicuously. The occasion presented itself during the quarterly collective social gatherings they had in the senior ministerial staff club which the minister usually attended, and which all directors and deputy directors were expected to attend. First, he had to get the poison. After several days of discreet inquiries, he was directed to a certain Malam Bouba in Briqueterie. He was apprehensive the night he went to see Bouba. He hoped the man would not ask too many questions. To his utmost relief, the only question Bouba asked him was whether he wanted "slow" or "instant" poison. After Bouba explained the difference between the two he settled for the second kind of poison.

"It's quite deadly," Bouba warned him as he gave him the yellow powder in a plastic wrapping. "This is just two grams, but it will kill an elephant in forty-five minutes. It will cost you one hundred thousand francs. It's most effective when you drop it an enemy's drink. One more thing before you go," Bouba added as Saddi stood up to leave, "this meeting never took place. I don't know you and I've never seen you before."

At first Saddi thought of paying Esomba, the barman, the sum of two hundred and fifty thousand francs to slip the powder in the director's drink. But he thought against it. If there was an investigation, Lucasi's death will be traced to him. No, he would do it himself. The following Friday was the quarterly social gathering. The minister, by tradition, would attend the occasion. Usually the minister only stayed for an hour or so and always made a speech, thanking the staff for their cooperation, hard work, and assiduity. And he left soon after the routine speech. Most directors would leave the gathering shortly after the minister's departure.

There was enough to eat and drink that Saturday evening. The minister was ushered into the hall at about 8 PM. He shook hands with the directors and sat down. Saddi moved close to where Lucasi was sitting ten minutes before the minister began his address. During one of the handclapping intervals, Saddi slipped the powder in Lucasi's drink. After the minister's customary speech Lucasi filled his half-empty glass and drank from it. Saddi moved away from the table and walked over to the bar. Five minutes later, the minister stood up to leave. He was ushered out of the hall by his bodyguard.

A few minutes after the minister left, Lucasi too stood up to leave. Saddi heaved a sigh of relief. He hoped for God's sake that the powder Bouba had given him would be effective.

News of Lucasi's death reached the ministry the next day. The minister sent a memo to all senior personnel in the ministry just after midday. The director had been involved in a car accident as he drove home from the ministerial staff club. Apparently, he had lost control of his car and crashed against a concrete electric pole. He was dead before the ambulance reached the hospital. It was most likely to be a heart attack. His funeral programme was going to be issued in due course.

Two weeks later, the ministry hired five buses that transported mourners from Yaoundé to attend the funeral in Lucasi's hometown. The wake took place in Lucasi's luxurious mansion in Batibo. As the mourners filed past the casket to catch a last glimpse of the dead man, they were horrified to see his eyes wide open. Saddi stood on the long line that inched forward slowly to have a last look at the illustrious director who had been snatched away by death at the prime of his youth. It was now Saddi's turn to walk up to the open casket. He took a step closer and looked at Lucasi's face. He was horrified to see Lucasi's eyes staring back at him in a fixed, cold glassy gaze. A chilly shudder ran down his spine. Even after he made the sign of the cross and walked out of the room, Lucasi's eyes stayed with him. He shook his head several times after the burial to shake off the stare of those frozen glassy eyes, but he couldn't. The invisible eyes were like the ubiquitous stare of a grandfather's enlarged photograph. They followed him wherever he went.

In an evocative eulogy during the requiem mass in the overcrowded Catholic Church, the parish priest paid tribute to the deceased director, stating how dedicated, honest, and patriotic he had been. The minister finally decorated the dead man with a posthumous presidential medal of valour. Lucasi was buried in the Catholic cemetery after the long mass. The funeral celebration itself with its elaborate masquerade dances and firing of guns was a lavish carnival with so much food and imported wine to drink that everyone in Batibo got drunk after the interment.

One item the *Cameroon Tribune* did not mention in its report of the director's obsequies was the strange incident concerning Lucasi's eyes that refused to close after his death. Even before Lucasi's corpse was removed from the mortuary, doctors at the Reference hospital administered all kinds of injections to relax his eyelids so that they could be closed, but the director's eyes refused to close. Specialists and morticians in New York, London, and Paris were contacted by phone and over the Internet, and drugs were sent by DHL to the Yaoundé Reference hospital in whose mortuary the director's corpse was kept. None of the prescriptions was effective. On the day of the removal of the corpse at the mortuary, the coffin was kept closed until Lucasi's mortal remains were conveyed to his hometown.

Saddi was relieved that Lucasi's eyes had faded away from his consciousness when he returned from the burial in Batibo. He got married to Bijanga a month after Lucasi died. They opted to make the marriage a low-key affair, inviting only a close circle of friends for the vows at the town hall. The reception took place at Saddi's newly built duplex in Ngousso. Saddi was appointed interim director of salaries in the ministry two months after their wedding. Then just barely a week after his new appointment, Lucasi's eyes appeared again to him.

One afternoon the minister was surprised when he received a letter from Saddi to the effect that he would prefer to occupy his present office until another office was found for him. It was a one-page rambling letter that the minister could not understand. The more the minister read the letter, the more confused he was. He called Saddi and told him to see him at 4 PM.

Saddi was ushered into the minister's cabinet at exactly 4 PM. The minister asked him to sit down and went straight to the point. "*Monsieur* Tegene, I don't understand the contents of your letter, that's why I called for you."

"I thought the letter was explicit, Mr Minister," Saddi responded.

"To you, perhaps. But not to me. We try as much as possible to be understood in administration. What do you mean by 'waiting for another office space to be created'? What office space are you talking about? You are expected to occupy your new office of director of salaries. If it's the office furniture you want changed, we'll change everything, including the carpet and curtains. There's a budget allocated for that."

"It's not that, sir. What … what I mean to say is that I don't want to move into the late director's office."

The minister was bewildered. "But why? It will be ridiculous for your subordinates or anyone looking for the director of salaries to find you in the deputy director's office. It will attract unusual attention to this ministry. This country being what it is, rumours will start circulating in the private press. It can even jeopardise my position as minister."

"Can't the office be moved into another room?"

"Definitely not, *Monsieur* Tegene. You know it can't be

moved. There're no other rooms on the fourth floor. Could you try and explain to me what this is all about?"

"Well, sir, it's … it's difficult to explain." He did not know how to tell the minister about his experiences. The minister would think he was losing his mind.

The minister kept quiet for a few moments. "It's about Lucasi, the deceased director, isn't it? I'm sure you were not in good terms with him. Well, we all knew he practiced the dark arts. I think that's what probably killed him. To be honest with you, and this is quite confidential, I didn't like him at all. I was scared of him. It's been a relief to all of us that he's no longer here. I'll approve the budget for furnishing the director's office tomorrow. I'll get the DGA to get interior decorators refurbish your office in less than three weeks, you understand?"

"Thank you very much, sir."

"Not at all. Our discussion this afternoon should remain private and confidential," the minister said as he stood up. He saw Saddi out into the secretariat before he came back to his cabinet.

Saddi moved into his new office with trepidation even after the office was completely renovated. The blank stare of those glassy eyes became more intensive after he moved into the refurbished office. It was by a share effort of will that he entered the office each morning to sit down on the director's chair and get on with the routine work in the ministry. He felt Lucasi's eyes watching him, staring over his shoulders as he worked on the numerous files on his desk. He could feel Lucasi's presence in the room as soon as he stepped into the office every morning. Sometimes, in the middle of the day, towards noon, his mind went blank. On two occasions, he had the strange feeling that he was actually Lucasi. He shook his head violently and almost dislocated his neck. Was Lucasi trying to take over his body? He became listless and began losing concentration on his job.

One afternoon, the intensity of Lucasi's eyes was so strong that he began sweating. He felt a strange tingling sensation on his scalp. All of a sudden that peculiar smell that had emanated from the spider's web that Sunday morning when he visited Lucasi's house in Bastos overpowered his nostrils. The odour was so insidious that it began suffocating him. He stood up from his swivel chair and staggered toward one of the upholstered chairs in the room. He started feeling dizzy and lost focus as he collapsed on the carpet in the middle of the room. It was at that moment that his secretary, *Madame* Biwole entered the office. She screamed when she saw him lying prostrate on the carpet.

"*Monsieur Le Directeur*!" She was so perplexed and confused that she did not know what to do.

"It's the smell!" Saddi muttered. "I can't stand it any longer!"

"What smell, Monsieur Le Directeur? Are you okay?"

"The eyes. Can't you see them? I can't stand them any longer."

"What are you talking about, *Monsieur Le Directeur*?"

"Lucasi's eyes." He struggled to rise to his feet.

"But Lucasi is dead, *Monsieur Le Director*. I think I should call for an ambulance."

He looked up and seemed to notice *Madame* Biwole for the first time. "An ambulance? What for? Oh, *Madame* Biwole. It's you. No, no, I'm okay." He rose to his feet slowly and struggled to sit on a nearby chair. "I had a terrible

headache and I blanked out momentarily. What was I saying?
I hope I didn't say anything strange or silly."

"No, *Monsieur*, you didn't. I think you should go home,
Monsieur. I'm sure you're overworked. This new job of director has been too hard on you. You need to see your doctor
and get a medical rest."

"You can go back to your secretariat now, *Madame*
Biwole. I was expecting to receive visitors from two thirty.
Please, cancel all my appointments. Tell them I'm indisposed."

"I will do that, *Monsieur*." *Madame* Biwole excused herself
and walked out of the cabinet.

Saddi went home earlier than usual that afternoon. When
Bijanga came back from work at four pm, she was surprised to
see his car parked in the garage and to find him at home. He
did not tell Bridget the incident in his office but mentioned
that he was not feeling well. The next day he went to see Dr
Clement Tembe, their family doctor.

"I can't find anything wrong with you," Dr Tembe said.
"I'll give a two-week medical rest. I suppose it's the stress of
work in your ministry. Here, this is a multivitamin prescription. You can buy it in any pharmacy. Take it easy on yourself."

When Bijanga got home in the evening, Saddi showed her
the multivitamin he had bought and the doctor's prescription
for a medical rest. He told her he would prefer to go to Buea
and spend the two weeks of his medical rest in the SJC guest
house. The climate at the foot of the mountain would be quite
helpful. Bijanga did not object. She thought getting out of
Yaoundé for two weeks will do him a lot of good.

Saddi was received by the young attendant who was in
charge of the mission guest house when he got to SJC on
Friday evening. The young man took his small suitcase into

one of the guest rooms. He had a cold shower, brushed his teeth and changed clothes. He was filled with nostalgia of his secondary school days when he came out on the balcony and sniffed the frosty mountain air. He walked over to the priests' residence. The priests he knew when he was a lad in the college had all retired or moved to other parishes, but Rev. Father Flynn had chosen to stay in the college. He had retired as a priest many years ago but had opted not to return to Ireland but live the rest of his days in the parish which he had pioneered. At sixty-eight he had a weather-beaten face and had developed a stoop on the shoulders; but he still looked strong and alert. Saddi was pleasantly surprised that Father Flynn could recognise him after all the years that had gone by.

"Well, well," Father Flynn said in his peculiar Irish accent, "if this isn't Saddi Tegene then I'm a bloody old man."

"Good evening, Father. Yes, it's me. You still have a wonderful memory, Father."

"Of course I do." They shook hands. "How long ago were you here at SJC?" Father Flynn inquired. "Class of '82?"

"No, Father. Class of '84. Your memory has failed you on this one."

"Auw damn it!" Father Flynn swore. "I always recognize the faces and names, but not those bloody graduating years. Well, well, it's auwfully nice to see you again. You're a director in one of the ministries in Yaoundé, I hear."

"Yes, Father. Director of salaries in the ministry of finance."

"So many hills, that Yaoundé. Can't figure out one section of the city from the other the few times I've been there. Streets are full of garbage, choked with motorbikes, yellow cabs, and exhaust fumes," Father Flynn carried on. "Bloody auwful place." He invited Saddi into the residence for tea and homemade biscuits the cook had baked. "So what brings you back to SJC?"

"I've taken two weeks off to have some rest. The guest house here and the mountain climate will do my frayed nerves a lot of good. My job has been rather stressful of late."

They climbed up a short flight of stairs and got to the priests' living room. Father Flynn waved him to a chair. He called the two other priests and introduced Saddi. The elderly priest, a native of Kumbo, shook hands with him and said, "Father Flynn has mentioned your name a number of times. Glad to meet you," while the younger man introduced himself as Father Neba from Bafut.

Saddi is of the Class of '82," Father Flynn said. "He's now a bloody big director in Yaoundé."

"Class of '84," Saddi corrected him. "Age is catching up on you, Father."

Both priests laughed as they sat down. The cook came from the kitchen and served tea with homemade tea biscuits. The four men talked about the college and life in general as they ate the biscuits and sipped their tea. Twenty minutes later, after the tea session was over, the two priests stood up and retired to their quarters.

After the two priests left, Father Flynn looked closely at Saddi's face. For the first time he noticed that Saddi looked pale and depressed. "There's something worrying you, isn't there? You look nervous and terrified of something."

"Yes, Father. That's why I've come here."

"You're not the only one. A lot of Christians come here to rest. The monastic atmosphere here has calmed many a troubled soul."

"Father," Saddi said, "my mind is burdened by a terrible deed."

"You want us to talk about it now?"

"No, Father, I want to confess my sins."

"I see. I'm scheduled to be at the confession box tomorrow. I'll wait for you in the chapel at 4 PM."

"Thank you, Father. I'll be there. I'll go to my room now. I'm tired. I need to rest." He stood up. Father Flynn too stood up. They left the room, came out on the corridor, and walked down the stairs together in silence. Father Flynn left him at the bottom of the staircase, wished him goodnight and returned to the residence. Saddi crossed the small lawn separating the priests' residence from the guest house. He entered the guest house, went to his room, and went to bed twenty minutes later.

He had hardly fallen asleep when he saw Lucasi's face. Lucasi's glazed eyes were red with antagonism. They looked threatening. "What do you want?" Saddi asked Lucasi. "You're supposed to be dead." The mouth on Lucasi's face was grim and firm. The eyes did not blink. They stared at him blankly. Saddi woke up with a start. He was sweating profusely and there was a heavy weight on his chest. He realized that he was having palpitations. He put on the light and looked at the time. It was two thirty in the morning. Was this the beginning of a heart attack? Perhaps he needed medical attention. He wondered whether he should go and wake up Father Flynn and tell him he was not feeling well. After a while, his heartbeat became regular again. Lucasi's eyes appeared each time he tried to sleep. He tossed and turned on the bed the whole night. The eyes would not leave him alone. It was around four in the morning that he managed to catch a light sleep.

He had breakfast on Saturday morning at 8 AM. Then he started moving round the college campus watching the students as they went about their Saturday tasks. He walked from one dormitory to another. First, he went up to St. Francis dormitory where he had lived when he was first admitted into Form One. After that he went to Bishop Rogan's dormitory before he came down to a group of dormitories they called 'the colonies' in those days. The building that housed the infirmary was still there. Mrs Kandem, the students' nurse, had died many years ago. The old refectory had been demolished and a new one had been built in its place. The only other new building was the ultramodern library the college alumni had built that housed the computer centre and Internet facilities. He felt as if he was one of the students walking around the campus. He wondered what life was really all about. He tried to imagine all the experiences in his days at SJC. Where had they gone to? Indeed, he had grown up and become a man. But paradoxically, he felt he was one of the students walking around the campus. The moment he had come out of the hired taxi and stepped into the college campus with his suitcase, time had unwound itself. He was now an SJC student again, admitted in September 1979. Was time real? Was it an illusion or was it merely a thief that played hide and seek with human memory? He knew time could not exist without memory. But it was human memory that gave meaning to time and life. He was so engrossed in his reflections that he lost track of where he was and what he was doing. He remembered hearing the sound of a gong. Yes, the refectory bell. Lunch time. How could he have forgotten? He found himself wandering towards the refectory. Students were entering the dining hall. He looked at his watch. It was fifteen minutes past midday. He approached one of the senior students and introduced himself as an old boy, class of '84. The boy was excited. He called the refectory prefect and introduced Saddi. The refectory prefect invited him to come and have lunch with the students in the dining hall. Saddi insisted that he would prefer not to be introduced. The prefect said that was okay. All of a sudden, talking and mingling with these youngsters gave him some zest for life, a purpose for living. He was filled with nostalgia when he came out of the refectory. He went back to the guest house at two fifteen for a brief siesta.

At about four fifteen he strolled over to the chapel. He came in through a side door, genuflected and made the sign of the cross before he walked towards the vestibule, turned left and entered the cubicle that contained the confession box.

He knew it was Father Flynn who was at the other side of the box. He knelt down, made the sign of the cross and said, "Bless me Father, I have sinned."

"God bless you, my child." Father Flynn's voice resonated from the other side of the cubicle. He heard the muffled rustle of his cassock as Father Flynn lifted up his right hand and blessed him with the sign of the cross. "When was your last confession?"

"I don't remember, Father."

"You're still a good Catholic, a faithful Christian, aren't you?"

"I am, Father. I don't attend mass regularly, but I go to church now and then."

"It's the weakness of the flesh," Father Flynn carried on. "You do receive Holy Communion, I'm sure"

"I do, Father."

"That's what's important. The body and blood of our Lord Jesus Christ in whom our salvation is guaranteed."

"I have committed a terrible sin, Father."

"A mortal sin?"

"Yes, Father."

"Fornication, Adultery? Embezzlement? Did you misappropriate money in the ministry?"

"No, Father. Anger. Jealousy. I … I killed Lucasi."

"Veke Lucasi? The deceased director?"

"Yes, Father."

"But he died of a heart attack. He had a car accident on his way home from a party. That's what the papers reported."

"I poisoned him in the party, in the staff club."

"But why? Why did you do it?" Father Flynn paused for a moment. This was a confession, not a cross examination, he reminded himself. His human curiosity was tempting him to find out the man's motive for extinguishing a mortal life. No, he would not do that. God was merely using him as an instrument to calm a troubled soul. "We're all sinners in the eyes of God. Unburden your heart to Christ who carried our sins on the cross of Calvary."

"I feared Lucasi, Father. I hated him. I was compelled to do away with him."

"Hate is legitimate. You can't like all men. Even St. Paul in the book of Romans says 'If it be possible, as much as lieth in you, live peaceably with all men.' But to take away another life, that's a different matter."

Saddi bowed his head and remained silent for a moment. He raised his head and said, "I had no choice, Father."

"You have sinned greatly, my son."

Father Flynn glanced at his watch. The confession session was approaching ten minutes. He leaned forward towards the small communication aperture. "You will do five hundred Hail Marys and two hundred and fifty glories to the Father on your rosary."

"I don't have a rosary, Father."

"I'll give you one."

As he raised his hand for the final benediction Father Flynn heard Saddi say, "It's not just repentance that brought me here, Father. I need God's protection."

"Protection? You already have His protection. The blood of Christ will save you from whatever hell you've created in yourself."

"Not from hell, Father. From ..." he hesitated.

"From what then?"

"From Lucasi, Father."

"Veke Lucasi? But he's dead."

"He's not dead, Father. He's alive. I know it. He's been tormenting me. I see him almost every day now."

"Your safety lies in the Blessed Virgin Mary. You committed a heinous crime, a mortal sin. Repent and you'll be saved."

"You don't understand, Father. I need help."

"What in Christ's name are you talking about?" Father Flynn felt himself getting irritated. The whole thing sounded strange and bizarre. Saddi obviously needed psychiatric attention, not a confession. But it was not his place to tell him. And this was not the appropriate place to tell a man that he needed psychiatric treatment, not divine salvation. When he spoke again there was a trace of impatience in his voice. "One hundred additional Hail Marys will free you from this torment."

"But his eyes, Father. His blank eyes keep gazing at me. I can't get rid of them. They follow me wherever I go. I see them at work, when I'm driving home, even when I'm asleep."

"Look," Father Flynn said, "there's no burden Christ can't bear." He was becoming exasperated. "You only need faith."

"Lucasi is trying to seek revenge, Father. He was a black magician."

"Lucasi? A black magician?"

"Yes, Father. During the past four days, he's been appearing to me in the shape of a spider, but his head and face are human."

"Good Lord, Mr Tegene! This is a confession, not an exorcising session. What's happened to your faith in God and the Church?"

"I'm a practicing Christian, Father, and I believe in God."

"Then for Christ's sake have faith in God and get hold of yourself!"

"Yes Father, I've heard. I'm sorry, Father." He used the back of his right hand to wipe away two streams of tears that were rolling down his cheeks.

"Go in peace my son, do your penance, and sin no more." Father Flynn crossed himself and executed a hasty blessing across the confessional orifice. 'In the name of the Father, and of the Son, and of the Holy Spirit, Amen.' He heard Saddi mutter 'Amen' as he stood up. The confession had exhausted him.

He came out of the confession cubicle and met Saddi at the vestibule. Saddi's head was bowed. His shoulders had assumed a stoop. Father Flynn feigned a cough to attract his attention. When Saddi looked up, Father Flynn said. "Remind me to give you a bottle of Holy water before you travel to

Yaoundé. Sprinkle it around your bed every night before you go to sleep. Here, have this rosary."

"Thank you, Father."

Father Flynn exited the chapel through a side door. Saddi went towards the altar, genuflected, and made the sign of the cross. He walked over to one of the benches and knelt down. He rolled the rosary around in his fingers and located the silver cross. He looked at the small cross momentarily before he crossed himself with it. He lowered his right hand and started rolling the beads with his thumb and index fingers to begin his penance.

He woke up on Sunday morning feeling restful and relieved. After his penance he returned to his room in the guest house feeling different. The confession had indeed helped him. For the first time in several days he had a restful night. Lucasi had not appeared to him. Lucasi's damned bloody spirit that was lost on its way to hell was scared of the reverend Fathers and the atmosphere in the chapel. This was holy ground. Father Flynn may have been right after all. No, he didn't have enough faith. If he had faith as much as a grain of mustard seed, was it Mathew 17, verse 20, he could chase away Lucasi himself. He attended mass with the students in the college chapel. It was Father Neba, the young priest who celebrated the mass. The students' neat uniforms, the harmonious melody of their singing, the bright sunlight after the church service, and the confession the previous day had lifted his spirits and lightened his guilt. Every night before he went to sleep in the guest house, he prayed with the rosary and sprinkled the Holy Water Father Flynn had given him on his body and around the bed. He spent each other day praying alone in the college chapel. He put himself on a partial fast, skipping breakfast and lunch and only eating in the evening at the guest house restaurant. He needed to build up his faith.

Saddi returned to Yaoundé after two weeks. He showed Bijanga the Holy water and told her what Father Flynn had said. He prayed with the rosary every morning when he got up from bed, and in the evening before he slept. He also carried the rosary and Holy water to his office.

Barely two weeks after Saddi returned from Buea, his momentary tranquillity from Lucasi's visitations was shattered. Lucasi's eyes appeared on Monday morning as soon as he entered his office and sat down. This time the glassy human eyes were gone. They were now replaced by the diminutive beady eyes of the black spider. He was even more frightened when he discovered thick strands of wool-like spider web under his chair on Monday morning when he went to work. He ordered the chair to be changed immediately. What had happened to Father Flynn's Holy water and the prayers with the rosary? He had not skipped a day without praying. Was this not faith? What had gone wrong? No, it was not his faith. It was Lucasi. He had used this brief interlude to reinforce his dark powers. This was a full-scale assault on his faith. He told Bijanga that he had traced his health problems to someone in the ministry who wanted his position as director of salaries. Bijanga convinced him that they should join a fundamental Apostolic prayer group in a small church not too far away from their house at Ngousso to wage war on the enemy in the ministry. They dismissed their two drivers and began using one car. Bijanga usually left work much earlier than Saddi, so they decided that she should use the Toyota Prado to pick him up from the ministry each day. Then they drove to the church for the prayer sessions and went back home only after 2 AM. On Saturday nights they had all night prayer vigils in the small church till the early hours of dawn when they went home for breakfast. The pastor of the Apostolic Church, Pastor Ebenezer Maduka, eventually convinced them to abandon their Sunday worship at the Catholic Cathedral in *Mvolye* and join his congregation.

One Friday night, in the early hours of the morning, Lucasi's face appeared again to Saddi. The glassy eyes on the human face were now small luminous beads dangling on a spider's head. Saddi was thrashing around on the bed, struggling to say something, when Bijanga woke up and switched on the light. Her husband's face was contorted in utmost pain and terror. She shook him several times, but she could not wake him up. He continued moaning. He seemed to be struggling with something or someone. For a moment Bijanga stopped shaking him. She had perceived an unusual sound. She bent down her head and listened. Yes, it was his heartbeat. It was so loud that she could hear it. This was not normal. She saw him clutch his chest. She rushed to the bathroom and brought the Holy water. She splashed some of the water on his face. That was when he woke up.

"My chest," he whispered, "oh my chest." The upper part of his pyjamas shirt was soaked in sweat. His heart was beating irregularly. "Palpitations. I'm having palpitations." Even as he spoke, the palpitations began dying down. His heartbeat became regular again after a few minutes. "I think I am okay. I feel much better."

He thought he should tell Bijanga what was happening to him, that Lucasi's face was no longer human but was now a gigantic spider's head with bright beady eyes dangling from it. No, he would not tell her. She would probably ascribe what he was experiencing to his jealous nature and Lucasi's rivalry to marry her when he as alive. Bijanga switched off the sidelight and they went back to sleep.

Bijanga called Dr Ako Tambe, their family physician, at 6:30 AM to fix an appointment for her husband at 10 AM. She made him a light toast at seven-thirty while he had a warm shower. After he finished dressing he ate the toast with marmalade and drank green herb tea without sugar. She refused to eat. She said she had no appetite. She noticed that his face was emaciated and his jaws were sunken in. When he finished his breakfast, she drove him to Dr Tambe's private clinic. They did not speak during the ten minutes' drive to the clinic. There were other patients waiting in the reception room when they got to the clinic, but the nurse ushered them into Dr Tambe's consultation office. Dr Tambe was not just their personal physician; he was a close family friend.

"Hey, what's wrong with you Saddi?" Dr Ako Tambe asked. A stethoscope hung down the right pocket of his white lab coat.

"He had an irregular heart beat last night," Bijanga responded.

"Could you please take off your clothes and lie down on the couch?" Dr Tambe told Saddi.

Bijanga sat on a chair while Saddi undressed. He climbed on the couch as Dr Tambe fastened the stethoscope to his ears. He bent down and began examining Saddi. He placed the stethoscope on his lower and upper chest and his back. Then he pressed Saddi's stomach with his two hands several times before he straightened up.

"You can put on your clothes. I've not detected anything

unusual." He went round to his table as he spoke. "I'll recommend further tests." He wrote on a small note pad. "You can do the tests at the Central or Reference hospital." He peeled off the paper and gave it to Bijanga. "I'll be hesitant to suggest that Saddi had a mild heart attack. It's only after these tests that I can make a definite judgement." Saddi finished dressing and thanked Dr Tambe as they went out of his office.

* * *

Because Saddi was tired and exhausted, they stayed at home the whole day watching news on CNN and The God channel. It was Bijanga who suggested that they stay away from the all- night vigil until the test results were out. They went to bed early that night after a light dinner, but Saddi could not fall sleep. He kept on turning and tossing in the bed the whole night. It wasn't till two thirty in the morning that he finally fell asleep.

He had hardly fallen asleep for ten minutes when he found himself driving his Toyota Prado on a remote highway. The road was a flat black ribbon of winding hills that disappeared in the distance beyond the ever-receding trees in the horizon. He could not remember how he got here or how long he had been driving. The only thing he remembered was seeing the name Bafia written on one of the road signs. All of a sudden, his consciousness became lucid. Yes, he was driving to Bamenda. Bafia was now sixty kilometres away and the dashboard clock showed the time to be six-thirty. He changed gears and switched on his headlights as he stepped hard on the accelerator. He wondered when he will get to Bamenda. It was that damned tyre repair that had wasted so

much of his time at Bafia. The young mechanic had told him
he shouldn't worry, that he will change the tyre in no time
and repair the one with the puncture. After that he would
have a smooth ride for the rest of the long drive to Bamenda.
He wondered whether he should drive on through the night.
He hated night driving. The blinding glare of headlights from
on-coming cars always left him dazed on the highway. Not
too long ago, in one of the local papers, he had read about
highway robbers ambushing motorists on lonely stretches
of the Bafia-Bamenda highway.

But he decided to drive on. Darkness was fast approaching. The engine groaned as the car picked up speed. It was
close to seven pm when he became aware that the car was
shuddering. He had perceived a slight jerking of the car
during the last five minutes, but his mind was too focused
on getting to Bamenda. He only became aware of the jerking
when he changed to fourth gear on the steep hills going up
to Banganté. He slowed down to third gear, thinking he was
over-straining the engine. After negotiating the next bend,
the engine shuddered violently and ceased abruptly. Saddi
managed to steer the decelerating car to the edge of the road
before it came to a final standstill. He came out, walked up
to the front of the car, and opened the engine compartment.
He peered at the engine for a few moments before he realised
that he could not see properly. He went back to the car and
came back with a flashlight. He switched it on and examined
the engine. There seemed to be nothing wrong with it.

The spark plugs, he thought. They must be worn out.
Nonsense! His mechanic in Yaoundé had changed the plugs
three days before this trip to Bamenda. A five-minute scru-
tiny of the engine yielded no clue to the unexpected engine

failure. Suddenly his mind flashed to the fuel tank. Yes, fuel! He went back to the car and cranked the engine, but the car would not start. It didn't matter. He had 20 litres of extra fuel in the jerry can in the car's trunk. He came out of the car, went to the trunk and opened it. It was empty. The jerry can was not there. Only the spare wheel and the tool box gazed mockingly at him. That was when he remembered what had happened at the filling station in Bafia where the young mechanic had repaired the leak on his left rear tyre. Yes, he had left the jerry can in Bafia. He visualised the smiling face of the young mechanic quite well.

"Will you go too far, sir?"

"No. I just want to have a drink and buy some extra batteries for my flashlight in the store across the road. The mechanic was removing the jack, the jerry can, and the spare tyre from the trunk as he began crossing the road. "I'll be back in ten minutes." He could not remember seeing the jerry can in the trunk when he came back and paid for the tyre change and repair job. Bafia was now about sixty kilometres behind.

He now remembered how Bridget had persuaded him not to travel that Thursday. She had woken up in the middle of the night, trembling and sweating profusely. Saddi thought she was sick. "What's the matter, sweetheart?" he asked her.

"I had a nightmare," she said, "a terrible dream. I don't think you should travel tomorrow, Saddi. You can leave for Bamenda on Friday morning, not tomorrow. Please."

"But I have to be in Bamenda on Thursday," he told her. "I have scheduled a meeting with the finance personnel in the delegation on Friday. I absolutely have to leave for Bamenda tomorrow afternoon.

"But the dream, Saddi ... the dream—"

"What dream? What are you talking about?"

"I've been having the same dream for the past three days. The cottage in the woods … the light in the dark … the dead man."

"O come on Bridget, it's your imagination—"

"It's real Saddi. It's been the same, each night. Please, darling, do not travel to Bamenda. Call Bamenda and cancel the meeting. Schedule it some other week."

"You think I've got some other woman in Bamenda? A girlfriend?"

"Oh, come on, Saddi. Stop thinking like this."

"Well then. You've been having bad dreams. Dreams have nothing to do with reality. Please go back to sleep. I have a busy day tomorrow morning."

"It's the dead man I see in the dream, Saddi. He … he looks exactly like you."

Saddi laughed nervously. "It's your imagination, darling." He kissed her lightly and switched off the bedside light.

He closed the trunk with a bang and thought of what to do. Should he sleep in the car? Perhaps he would be lucky if another vehicle came along. He entered the car and closed the door. He made up his mind to sleep in the car till morning. He was about adjusting the car seat to a comfortable position when he noticed a distant light in the surrounding forest. He came out of the car just to be sure. Yes, it was a light all right, but it was quite faint, to the right of the car. An occasional flicker caught his eye as the branches of the forest trees swayed under the gentle touch of a slight breeze. He estimated the distance from the road and placed it to be approximately three hundred metres.

He wound up the car's side screens and closed the doors

before he switched on the torch. He looked at his wristwatch. It was already to 8 PM. The rays of his flashlight picked up a narrow dirt road leading into the forest. A strong cold wind had replaced the gentle breeze that had been swaying the branches a few minutes ago. He began walking along the dirt path, his flashlight slicing a path through the intense darkness of the night with a vivid luminous glow. The thought of a hospitable house with a warm firewood fire where he would bask himself made him quicken his pace. The path snaked through the tall menacing trees and suddenly came out on a small lane with giant eucalyptus trees standing like silent sentries on both sides of the track. A ghastly wind rocked the quavering branches and an owl hooted somewhere nearby. The light ahead became brighter. Then he found himself at the end of the lane. The bright beam of his touch showed an old white fence with paint peeling from the fence boards and a broken gate. He swung his right hand skyward and the probing beam of the flashlight revealed the upper floor of an old country bungalow. He swung the flashlight in a circle and the light disclosed what appeared to be a dilapidated house with a small yard. He moved the flashlight again upwards, to the left, and saw a chimney, a broken window pane, and a sloping roof. He switched off the light and stood still. Not a sound. The single light he had seen from the road had suddenly been put off. Perhaps the inhabitants in the house were just about going to bed. He moved toward the gate. A thick overgrown hedge surrounded the bungalow. The broken wooden gate was the only entrance into the overgrown yard. One part of the gate collapsed when he pushed it. He moved up to the front door and knocked hard. He knocked the door again a second time with his left knuckles. He tried the door handle and to his surprise the door creaked open and swung inwards. He entered the house and closed the door behind him. The beam of his flashlight revealed the interior of the ground floor of the house. The room was chilly. The paint on the walls was peeling off and the windows were broken. A chilly shiver ran down his spine but he quickly threw the fear off his mind. Even if the house was uninhabited he would try and find somewhere he could lie down and pass the night. It was better in here than exposing himself to the dangers on the highway.

There was a staircase to his left leading upstairs. He walked to the staircase and began climbing upstairs. All of a sudden his heart began throbbing rapidly. He had the strange feeling that someone was watching his progress up the stairs. He felt that flutter of fear again in the pit of his stomach. The balustrades were coated by a thick layer of dust, so too were the old wooden stairs which creaked mournfully, more or less like laughter which reverberated in the whole house. He finally finished the stairs and alighted on a small corridor. Without warning his torch went out as if it had been extinguished by an invisible hand. He switched it on and off several times but it did not come on. For the first time in his life, Saddi felt cold fear creep up his spine and a strange tingling sensation on his scalp.

Before the flashlight went off he had noticed a door to his left. He groped forward in the darkness following the wall. The wall ended abruptly and he felt a door. He reached for the handle and tried it. The door swung open inwards as he entered a room. He did not hear the door close behind him when he stepped into the room. The moon had risen outside and its pale light streamed in through one of the broken windows. That was when he saw an indistinct silvery form in the middle of the room. He bent forward and touched it. He quickly withdrew his hand. He had touched an enormous spider's web. His ears caught the rustle of clothes behind him and he spun round. The rays of the moonlight from the window revealed the outline of a dark familiar face.

"Veke Lucasi!" Saddi whispered. "You can't be alive. You're dead! What are you doing here?" The rest of his words got stuck in his throat. He stepped behind, chilled with fear. He fell down and his head hit the wooden floor. Then he felt another strange sensation—he was being wrapped up in the thick woolly strands of the spider's web. Gripped now by an inevitable certainty of doom he began calling his wife's first name. "Bridget ... Bridget ..." A hand gripped his throat and forced his mouth open. Thick strands of spider web were thrust into his mouth. "Bridget ..." He was now struggling for breath. It was at that moment that a glowing radiance filled the room.

"Tonight the spider shall feed." It was Lucasi's voice. It was close, so close, whispering in his left ear.

"You're dead!" Saddi muttered. "You're dead!"

* * *

Bijanga woke up with a muffled scream in her throat. She got up quickly and put on the bedside lamp. Saddi was thrashing about on the bed and struggling to say something. His breathing was shallow and his chest was heaving up and down in a rapid desperate movement. Bijanga held him on the shoulders and shook him violently in an effort to wake him up. His eyes were turned upward and the lower part of

127

his jawbone was moving up and down as if he was being forced to chew or bite something against his will. Bijanga ran out of the bedroom, went to the telephone and called the emergency ambulance number. After that she called Dr Tambe. She ran back to the bedroom and found her husband lying quite still with his mouth half-open. She felt his pulse. It was irregular and beating faintly. She collapsed on her knees and began to pray. Five minutes later she heard the wail of the ambulance sirens. Dr Tambe's car got to the house before the ambulance. She heard him pounding the front door with his fist. She ran downstairs and opened the door. The first thing Dr Tambe said was "How bad is it?"

"I don't know, Doctor," Bijanga said. "He doesn't seem to be breathing. I felt his pulse a few minutes ago. It's quite faint."

Dr Tambe took the stairs two at a time, with Bijanga following at his heels. He stopped at the landing and waited for Bijanga to catch up with him. Bijanga turned left and Dr Tambe followed her into their spacious bedroom.

"Oh my God!" Dr Tambe exclaimed as soon as he saw Saddi. "There's no time to waste. Come on, let's place him on the floor."

He took hold of Saddi by the shoulders and Bijanga held his legs. They lowered him on the floor. The sirens of the ambulance sounded much closer. Dr Tambe began the CPR procedure, forcing his own breath into Saddi's mouth after every twenty seconds and pressing his folded hands on his chest. Even when he saw the flashing red lights of the ambulance in front of the house, he continued with the CPR as he struggled to resuscitate Saddi's heart.

"Go downstairs and tell them to bring the stretcher up here. He must be taken to the hospital at once. We need to get his heart going again."

Bijanga rushed downstairs and brought two of the paramedics upstairs. "We don't have much time," Dr Tambe barked out instructions. "We must get him to the Central Hospital in less than five minutes."

"Yes, doctor," one of the paramedics said.

The two paramedics lifted him from the floor and strapped him on the stretcher. As they began wheeling the stretcher out, one of the paramedics noticed something in Saddi's open mouth. "Doctor!" he said. "Doctor! Come and see! This is strange, very strange!"

Dr Tambe came to the stretcher and the paramedic pointed at Saddi's open mouth. "Look! In his throat. There's something inside. The two paramedics held open Saddi's mouth and Dr Tambe inserted two of his fingers into Saddi's throat. A moment later he pulled out thick strands of white spider web from Saddi's mouth. He inserted his fingers again in Saddi's throat and pulled out more spider web. The strands of spider web seemed to be deep inside his oesophagus.

"Where did this stuff come from? I haven't seen anything like this in my entire medical practice." He turned round and looked at Bijanga. There was a blank gaze on her face. She looked traumatized, unable to say anything or explain what was happening to her husband. "We need to get this man to the Central Hospital right away!" Dr Tambe shouted at the paramedics as they began wheeling the stretcher downstairs. "This is an emergency!"

No one saw the big black spider creep out of Saddi's mouth, crawl down the side of his face, and creep down the stretcher unto the floor before they reached the ambulance. Bijanga locked the front door and entered Dr Tambe's car.

Dr Tambe started the car and they followed the flashing lights of the ambulance as it wailed its way to the hospital. By the time the ambulance got to the Central Hospital, Saddi Tegene was declared DOA (dead on arrival) by doctors at the emergency unit.

* * *

Saddi's wake was on Friday December 14th, two weeks after his death in Yaoundé. The Ministry of Finance, as usual, hired five buses to convey the mourners to his hometown. Father Flynn, Father Neba, and the Rev. Father from Kumbo decided to take part in the requiem mass for the deceased director when they heard the funeral programme announced over the radio. The three priests introduced themselves to Rev. Father Francis Dopgima of the Batibo parish when they got to Batibo. Father Francis conceded the role of chief celebrant for the funeral mass to Father Flynn the moment he learnt that Father Flynn had been Saddi Tegene's principal at SJC.

Over the years, the overcrowded cemetery had expanded to additional inhospitable ground. As they searched for a spot to dig the late director's grave, the gravediggers complained about the stones and hard ground on the entire perimeter of the cemetery. The only available piece of land in the crowded burial ground, where there were no stones or hard ground, which the diggers found, was a small portion of land next to Lucasi's grave.

Saddi was laid to rest at four fifteen pm on Saturday the 15th. The altar boys placed the candles they had carried from the church on the ground surrounding the grave. After the final songs and prayers in the pervasive miasma of incense at the graveside, Father Flynn sprinkled Holy water on the coffin before the gravediggers lowered it gently into the grave. He scooped up a handful of earth and threw it on top of the lowered coffin. The earth hit the coffin with a dreary hollow thud that reverberated in the grave and resounded back to the ears of the mourners. It was at that moment that Dr Tambe saw a huge black spider emerge from under the coffin. It crawled slowly across the coffin and crept into a hole on the horizontal wall of Lucasi's grave. One by one, the other priests picked up the freshly dug earth and tossed it into the grave. Then it was the turn of the catechist, the altar boys, Hilda, close relatives, and friends of the deceased. Even as the mourners tossed the earth in the grave, one of the muscular grave diggers jumped into the grave and made a signal with his hand to his two friends above him. The two young men began excavating large chunks of fresh soil and shovelling them into the grave. They stopped after every five minutes or so to allow the man in the grave stamp the soil with his feet before they commenced shovelling the soil.

The mourners stood by, sobbing and watching as the grave steadily filled up. The three gravediggers, bare skin with only shorts for clothing, and the sweat dripping down their muscular chests, continued stamping the earth in a rhythmic dance of death. They harmonized the trampling of their feet with an orchestrated hum-chant that emanated from deep down their throats. The priests, catechist, and altar boys began leaving the cemetery. One by one, the rest of the mourners too began to disperse. Only Bijanga and her in-laws stood by, apparently hypnotized by the grave diggers' resonant chant and the regular trample of their bare feet on the grave.

Dr Tambe caught up with Father Flynn as the priests walked back to the Rev. Fathers' residence. "Tambe, Dr Ako Tambe," he introduced himself. "I was his family physician. I attended to him the night he passed away."

"I see. Glad to meet you," Father Flynn responded. "Aufully sorry I can't shake hands. Didn't know the damned bloody earth would be this sticky."

"Tell me Father," Dr Tambe continued, "did you see the big black spider that emerged from the soil and crawled across the coffin."

"Of course, I did."

"That was strange, wasn't it, Father?" Dr Tambe carried on.

"Perhaps," Father Flynn responded. "Why do you find it strange?"

"You don't find it strange, Father?"

"No, not really. It depends on your notion of what's strange."

"I see. What I mean is do you have underground spiders that big, tunnelling their way in cemeteries?"

"No, not that I know of," Father Flynn said. "Well, I'm not an arachnologist, you know. There should be some kind of explanation. Perhaps a species we don't know about."

"But the gravediggers would have seen it," Dr Tambe carried on. "I wonder how it can survive deep down six feet below the earth."

"I wonder," Father Flynn said, "I really wonder. What did you say your name was?"

"Tambe, Ako Tambe."

"You see, Dr Tambe, I try sometimes not to second guess

the ways of God or most often, as I've come to discover, the ways of the devil."

Dr Tambe was taken aback. "The devil?"

"Many strange things happen in life, doctor. Things we don't know. Things we can't explain."

"You think ... you think that spider ... is the work of the devil?"

There was an insightful grin on Father Flynn's weather-beaten face. "Could have been. But please, don't quote me. We'll never know the entire truth."

As they spoke, it began to rain. The initial showers changed into a steady, monotonous downpour. People began running to seek shelter from the rain. The burial and the dead man were momentarily forgotten as everyone scuttled around to escape the unanticipated torrential rainstorm.

ABOUT THE AUTHOR

B a'bila Mutia is an award-winning Cameroonian author, poet, and playwright. He holds an MA in Creative Writing from the University of Windsor, Canada. His short stories and poetry have been featured in anthologies and reviews worldwide. He is the author of *Whose Land?* (Longman children's fiction); "Rain" (short story) in *A Window on Africa*; "The Miracle" (short story) in *The Heinemann Book of Contemporary African Short Stories*; "The Spirit Machine" (short story) in *The Spirit Machine and Other New Short Stories from Cameroon*, *Coils of Mortal Flesh* (poetry) and *The Journey's End* (2016). In 1993, Mutia was a guest of the Berlin Academy of Arts for an international short story reading. In September 2011, Mutia's play, *The Road to Goma*, was among six winners of the African Playwriting Project sponsored by the London National Theatre Studio where excerpts of his play were staged by professional actors. He has lived in Lagos and Benin City (Nigeria), Windsor and Halifax (Canada). He currently resides in Yaoundé, Cameroon where he is professor of African literature and creative writing at the École Normale Supérieure.

ABOUT THE PUBLISHER

Spears Books is an independent publisher dedicated to providing innovative publication strategies with emphasis on African/Africana stories and perspectives. As a platform for alternative voices, we prioritize the accessibility and affordability of our titles to ensure that relevant and often marginal voices are represented at the global marketplace of ideas. Our titles – poetry, fiction, narrative nonfiction, memoirs, reference, travel writing, African languages, and young people's literature – aim to bring African worldviews closer to diverse readers. Our titles are distributed in paperback and electronic formats globally by African Books Collective.

Connect with Us

Visit our Website
Go to www.spearsmedia.com to learn about exclusive previews and read excerpts of new books, find detailed information on our titles, authors, subject area books, and special discounts.

Subscribe to our Free Newsletter
Be amongst the first to hear about our newest publications, special discount offers, news about bestsellers, author interviews, coupons and more! Subscribe to our newsletter by visiting www.spearsmedia.com

Quantity Discounts
Spears Books are available at quantity discounts for orders

of ten or more copies. Contact Spears Books at orders@
spearsmedia.com.

Host a Reading Group
Learn more about how to host a reading group on our
website at www.spearsmedia.com

Also by Ba'bila Mutia
The Journey's End

When Akuma—a youthful African government secondary school teacher—leaves his hometown and goes to the capital city, hardly does he know that he will be paralyzed and will not be able to use his legs again. The Journey's End is a character-driven narrative that explores the lives of two men who meet in Yaoundé, the capital city—Lucas Wango (an elderly pensioner who comes to collect his back pay of seven years' pension money) and Akuma (a physically challenged man who helps him recover his pension arrears). Wango doesn't know that Akuma, aka Général, is a mobster and the boss of a city gang that commands and controls a better part of the metropolis.

Running parallel to this central plot are two subplots that eventually converge at the end of the novel—Lucas Wango's meddling in and eventual frustration with national political life and Général's relationship with Martina, a woman he falls in love with in the city.

CPSIA information can be obtained
at www.ICGtesting.com
Printed in the USA
LVHW09191916112
733323LV00003B/474

9 781942 876700